PUFFIN BOOKS

OF REVOLUTIONARIES AND BRAVEHEARTS

NOTEABLE TALES FROM INDIAN HISTORY

'What's the point of learning about all these kings and wars?'

The refrain that puts most children off history, somehow didn't bother Mallika at all. Perhaps because she had her own quirky way of looking at the past. While maths and chemistry nightmares return to haunt Mallika even years after school, history only finds more meaning in her world. This book seeks to share that perspective with children who love history and with those who don't. For in the end, history is not about kings and wars. History is about finding out who you are!

Mallika has a master's degree in ancient Indian culture and history. You can find her articles, blogposts and podcasts at www.mallikaravikumar.com

OF REVOLUTIONARIES AND BRAVEHEARTS

NOTEABLE TALES FROM INDIAN HISTORY

*Finding Meaning
in Our Past*

MALLIKA RAVIKUMAR

Illustrations by Sai Mandlik

PUFFIN BOOKS
An imprint of Penguin Random House

PUFFIN BOOKS

USA | Canada | UK | Ireland | Australia
New Zealand | India | South Africa | China

Puffin Books is part of the Penguin Random House group of companies
whose addresses can be found at global.penguinrandomhouse.com

Published by Penguin Random House India Pvt. Ltd
4th Floor, Capital Tower 1, MG Road,
Gurugram 122 002, Haryana, India

Penguin
Random House
India

First published in Puffin Books by Penguin Random House India 2020

Text copyright © Mallika Ravikumar 2020
Illustrations copyright © Sai Mandlik 2020

ISBN 9780143446859

Book design by Akangksha Sarmah
Typeset in Adobe Caslon Pro by Manipal Technologies Limited, Manipal
Printed at Aarvee Promotions, India

www.penguin.co.in

To
Profs
Kurush Dalal, Prachi Moghe
Suraj Pandit & Shilpa Chheda

for helping me see
history differently.

CONTENTS

Contents

Contents

NOTE TO THE READER

This is a work of historical fiction intended for readers to gain a better appreciation of history.

Facts recorded in history are central to the stories.

Liberty has been taken with compressing time periods, introducing characters, adding dialogue and plot elements as required. The intent of the work is to provide you with a view of history such that it appears more relatable.

The two sections that follow every story—Connecting the Historical Dots and Unboxing the Past—provide perspective and historical information related to the story.

It is hoped that these stories will provide you, dear reader, with an alternative lens to look at history. The endeavour is to help you find meaning in the past, rather than look upon history as a dry-as-bone narrative of kings, dynasties, dates and wars.

STORIES
OF CLASS
AND
CONFLICT

THE SAINT OF PANDHARPUR

1

GOD IN A COPPER POT

'Get out of my way, you dirty creature!' screamed the old priest, charging towards Aruna.

'But . . . But . . .' Aruna muttered, making her way ahead of the crowd. 'I want to see Lord Vithoba and touch his feet. My mother . . .'

'Touch Vithoba's feet?' the old man thundered, turning up his nose. 'What impunity! What audacity! You lowly human beings have no business being here. You dogs pollute this temple by your mere presence. Get your filthy little self out of here at once!'

Aruna ran to her father at the back of the crowd, trembling in fear. Tears streamed down her cheeks as she threw her arms around him, unable to comprehend why the old man had yelled at her and made her feel so small.

'I did no wrong, Baba' cried Aruna. 'Why did the bhatji scold me?'

'Bala, it is not your mistake,' her father sighed, hugging her tightly. 'You are too young to understand . . . But listen to me this time, my child. Please, please I beg you . . . Do not try to enter the temple again.'

'But why not, Baba?' Aruna cried. 'How else will I pray to Vithoba for Aai's health,' she said between sobs, 'if I cannot enter the temple?'

'You can pray from here, little one. We all do. I'm sure Vithoba will hear your prayers, even from outside,' he said in a voice so small, it was barely audible.

'Then why come here at all?' asked Aruna, confused and suddenly angry, as she wiped her tears. 'Have we not travelled for days to Pandharpur in the scorching heat so that we may see Vithoba and pray to him? Did you not tell me that Vithoba would cure Aai of her illness if I asked him to make her all right?'

Tuka stared at his daughter blankly. Then drawing his three children silently by their little hands, he led them to the far end and settled atop a perching spot. All around them, as far as the eyes could see, were devotees in the thousands—the old and the young, the sick and the infirm, the disabled and the poor—with few to no possessions in hand but great faith at heart. Walking barefoot across Maharashtra in the blistering heat of May had worn them out. They were bedraggled and unkempt, tired and weary. But none of that kept them from chanting and singing praises of Lord Vithal, praying for their sorrows to be washed away.

'*Tell me* Baba, why can't we enter the temple?' Aruna begged.

Tuka could form no reply. Having visited Pandharpur every year for over two decades, he had never stepped inside the temple. Now, as he stood outside Vithal's abode in Pandharpur, beside his sons Vishnu and Narayan, looking into the eyes of his little girl who had trudged several miles with great faith and hope, he felt cheated and exhausted. Questions, for which he had no answers, began to churn within him. He had been told since he was only a child, that he was dirty. His touch, his sight, his mere presence. 'Mahar,' they called the likes of him. People whose presence, he was told, would pollute the temple and the Lord himself. He had grown accustomed to the humiliation. Grown accustomed to announcing his arrival as he walked the streets so the upper castes could maintain their distance. Grown accustomed to not daring to cross the invisible lines drawn around him. At temples. At wells. Everywhere.

'Baba! What in god's name are they doing?' gasped Vishnu, tugging at his father's dhoti, drawing him out from thoughts as he pointed to a group of priests, huddled together outside the temple. A large number of them, including Gopalshastri Gore, the authorized priest of the temple, had begun chanting mantras with great fervour, as huge pots of water were being carted into the temple from the Bhima River that flowed behind it.

'The *maha* pooja has begun!' screamed one of the younger priests, shooing away the crowds that thronged the gateway of the temple. Large earthen pots filled with water from the Bhima River were emptied over the idol of Vithal by the priests. Hurriedly, the pundits chanted and recited verses from the holy texts, *stripping* the idol of its divinity, which now rested in a small copper pot where water dripping from the idol was quickly collected. The copper pot was then speedily sealed and blessed by the head priest.

'Worship your Vithal now, you fools!' he laughed, mockingly. 'The real Vithal is safe elsewhere, protected from your polluted presence!' he muttered as he walked away.

Unable to comprehend, Aruna's Baba turned towards another onlooker. '*Mawli*! What is going on here?' he called to an old man, using the term devotees used to address one another.

'They wash the idol of Vithal to remove its divinity!' the old man laughed, hitting his head with his palms. 'So that it is not polluted by the presence of the lower caste like us!'

'*Ho ka?*' he said. 'Is that so?' Aruna's father looked bemused. 'Does the lord's divinity get washed away just like that?'

'Anything is possible in this world, Mawli! I have lived many long years. This spectacle was all I had left to see!' the old man sighed.

The black stone idol of Vithal, stood with its hands at its hips, a silent witness to the madness.

'God no longer vests in the stone idol,' hollered the high priest. 'This is the essence of the Lord!' he announced, holding up the pot for all to see. 'He is in this copper pot! And shall remain pure and unpolluted from the presence of you untouchables!' he barked, nostrils flaring.

Aruna stared in disbelief. *How could this be happening?* For weeks, she had walked along with the Varkaris, devotees of Vithal, singing the soulful *abhangs* of Tukaram and Dnyaneshwar, two of Maharashtra's most renowned saints, about how the world was one and all people were equal. For days she had travelled in the harsh heat, hoping that Vithal would cure her ailing mother in the village. For months she had dreamed of seeing the god who was hailed as the Saviour of All. And here she was witnessing something she could've never imagined.

'The idol is no longer divine!' the man roared. 'The Lord is in this copper pot and shall stay *safe* in my home. Away from your polluted gaze and touch! Now do what you will!' the high priest spat, as he addressed the shocked gathering outside the temple, before walking away in contempt.

The Varkaris watched in horror. Frozen in shock. Weeping in grief. Whispering their disapproval in hushed tones. Some spoke about the scriptures. Others about equal rights and reform.

Vishnu was old enough to be confused, and stood scratching his head. Narayan was too young to understand and fidgeted with a stick in his hand. But Aruna, unconcerned with worldly matters, was crying inconsolably. Her worries were more personal: If Vithoba was God no more, who would heal her ailing mother?

2

OBEDIENT DISOBEDIENCE

After the shock wore off, the crowds slowly moved south. Having nowhere else to go, Aruna and her Baba followed, and soon found themselves in a large hallway amidst hundreds of others staring at a frail old man, dressed in white. He sat at one end of the hall upon a straw mat. A few people were seated with him. A small group on his right were singing devotional hymns. Words of Sant Eknath and Tukaram . . . words that spoke of love and oneness.

A large crowd was milling about the hall. Nodding to familiar faces, Aruna's father made his way in, clutching her hand in his.

'A telegram . . . a telegram has arrived! From Gandhiji!' a young boy came running into the hall with great excitement. All eyes turned towards the boy. 'Guruji, a telegram has arrived from Gandhiji!' the young boy repeated, tearing open its contents.

Suddenly, a wave of excitement ran through the crowd. Everyone sat down in neat rows facing the front, eager to know what was going on.

'Read it,' the old man instructed the boy.

'Who is this man, Baba?' Aruna whispered, as they all waited for the telegram to be read.

'This, my dear, is Sane Guruji,' replied Tuka. 'He has been fasting for the last several days, to protest against the temple authorities for refusing to open the temple doors to people . . . like us.'

'Sane Guruji? You mean *the* Sane Guruji? The same Sane Guruji who has written *Shyamchi Aai* and *Miri*?' Aruna shrieked.

Her father smiled. 'Yes Bala, the same Sane Guruji who has written your favourite storybooks!'

Aruna's face lit up. She walked right up to the front of the hall so she could see the much-loved children's author clearly.

'What does it say, beta?' the frail voice of Sane Guruji was heard, imploring the young boy standing beside him. But upon looking at his ashen expression, Sane Guruji sensed that something was amiss. He looked around and caught sight of little Aruna, standing in front of him.

'Come here little one,' said Sane Guruji, calling out to Aruna lovingly.

Aruna hesitated, suddenly conscious of herself. 'Do you know how to read?' Guruji asked the girl. Aruna nodded shyly. 'Then won't you help me?' he smiled, gesturing towards the telegram. Aruna stepped forward and held the telegram in her trembling hands. About a hundred people were watching her. She could hear her heart beat. In her hand, was a message from Mahatma Gandhi!

Hesitantly, with a low voice, Aruna began reading.

'On . . . On . . . the facts before me . . . your fast . . . is wholly wrong.' A loud gasp from the crowd made her pause. Sane Guruji gestured her to continue. 'Pandharpur Temple will be opened shortly to Harijans. Your courage and greatness should dis . . . disdain tau . . . taunts of men however great or many. Please stop the fast and wire.'

A strange silence descended upon the hall. Aruna had not understood but she sensed the tension. Gandhiji had called Sane Guruji's fast wholly *wrong*. She was old enough to understand that much.

'I thought Gandhiji would support us!' an animated voice cut into the tense air from somewhere at the back.

'I feel heartbroken! I can't believe this!' whispered a bespectacled lad sitting near Sane Guruji.

Sane Guruji's face mirrored his disappointment. Gandhiji, he'd thought, would support him. Instead, the Mahatma had asked him to stop the fast. He was deeply hurt.

'Gandhiji has requested that you withdraw your fast,' remarked a middle-aged man, kneeling beside Sane Guruji. 'Won't you agree now? Please give up your fast . . .'

'Yes Guruji,' pleaded a woman sitting by his side. 'We are worried about you. Your health is getting worse with each passing day. You must eat. Our protests to have the temple opened to all will never stop! But not at this cost! Please Guruji . . . please give up your fast.'

'Please Guruji, please!' a chant of pleas arose from all around. Sane Guruji belonged to the priestly class. Yet, he felt the bite of injustice suffered by the untouchables. It had been nine days since he'd eaten. Could he give up now?

It was a strange situation: The lifelong dream of freedom was about to be realized. The British were leaving after having ruled for two centuries. India was at the cusp of freedom. Yet, was that freedom complete if the people were not truly free? Sane Guruji had made it his mission to have the temple doors opened to all. Even if it came at the cost of his life.

Listening to the chorus of voices around him, Guruji smiled. He gestured to Aruna to come and sit beside him, taking the telegram from her and peering at it. Aruna sensed the deep disappointment in his eyes as he surveyed its contents.

'What do you think, little one?' he whispered to Aruna.

Aruna stared at the floor, unable to look at Sane Guruji or the crowd before her.

'Don't be shy . . . tell me what you think,' smiled Guruji, pulling her towards him.

'My Aai . . .' Aruna began, hesitantly. 'My mother is sick,' she said, with a tear rolling down her cheek. 'I came here to pray for her. But now . . . now . . . they tell me I cannot enter the temple. Then they say they have washed his idol and Vithoba is no longer divine! How can that be? What will I do?' she hid her face in her hands and sobbed.

Guruji ran his hand affectionately over her hair and wiped her tears. 'How can Vithu refuse the prayers of a little angel like you?' his eyes lit up with a twinkle. Aruna gave a small smile; his warmth lit up her mood. 'Okay now . . . Gather all the children. I will tell you all a story!'

'But first . . . let me send Gandhiji a reply,' Guruji mumbled to himself, gesturing to the bespectacled boy to come near.

'Send a telegram to Bapu,' he said, as the young man pulled out a notepad. 'Tell him that I have been his ardent follower and devoted student all my life.' He closed his eyes, thinking, while the crowd seated in the hall waited with bated breath to hear his response.

'However,' Guruji closed his eyes, 'tell him that in this case, I can uphold the principles he has taught me only by disobeying him. The fast shall not be withdrawn.'

THE SAINT

'Do you know Chokhamela?' began Guruji lightly, once the reply to Gandhiji had been dispatched. The children seated around him shook their heads. 'Come! Let me tell you about the man who was fondly called Chokhoba!'

Having fasted so long, Guruji's voice was feeble and soft. They all gathered around him, as he cleared his throat to begin his tale.

'More than two hundred years ago, right here in Pandharpur, there lived a man named Chokhoba. He worked as a mason, building walls and houses. He was a great devotee of Vithoba and visited the temple every day. But he had a problem. Can you guess what that problem was?'

'He was poor and did not have any food?' Narayan said hesitantly. Guruji shook his head.

'Perhaps he was blind and could not see,' said an older girl sitting behind him. Guruji shook his head again.

'He was a Dalit and could not enter the temple,' said Aruna confidently.

Sane Guruji nodded.

'Chokha was a Mahar and so, he was not allowed into the Vithoba temple by the priests,' he said. 'He would stand outside the temple every day after he had finished his work, singing praises of the Lord, composing bhajans and abhangs. But even though the priests were rude to him, and wouldn't allow him into the temple, his faith never wavered. And then one day, something magical happened.'

The children inched closer to Guruji. Even the grown-ups listened in rapt attention. Sane Guruji was a master storyteller and even when he was on the ninth day of his fast, he could enthral listeners with his stories.

'One day,' continued Sane Guruji, 'Chokha had been standing at the door of the temple from morning, praying the entire day. The priests mocked him, laughing and taunting him by saying that the Lord's grace did not shine upon untouchables like him. They told him he was wasting his time and asked him to move away from the temple, as he was polluting the holy place with his presence. But Chokha did not budge. His faith was unshakeable. Deaf to their taunts, he stood outside the temple, deep in meditation, forgetting himself and his surroundings.'

'What happened then?' Vishnu asked eagerly. 'You said something magical happened to him! Tell us!'

'Yes, yes,' said Guruji and smiled, 'something magical indeed! At night, the devotees vacated the temple after the evening *aarti*, and the temple priests locked up the temple and left as usual. Chokha was still standing outside with his hands folded and eyes closed, deep in prayer. The priests ridiculed him as they made their way home. Unperturbed, Chokha stood his ground and called out to the Lord that he loved. 'My dear Vithu,' he cried, 'will you not give me your darshan just once? Do you not see how they insult me? Do you not hear how they taunt me? Do you have no love for me?'

Aruna closed her eyes. She could feel Chokhoba's pain. Anger bubbled up within her. She realized her father and mother and everybody else in her family had been treated like that for years. Why had they allowed themselves to be humiliated for so long? *Why Baba? Why did you tolerate these insults?* The question kept ringing out in her mind each time she looked into her Baba's face.

'So,' Sane Guruji continued, 'shunned by all, yet filled with faith and hope, Chokha stood outside the temple, alone and forlorn in the cold. Then suddenly, in the middle of the night, when everything else was still, the temple doors blew open all by themselves. Startled, Chokha opened his eyes! And there he saw it—his beloved Vithoba standing at the door. "Vithu! Is . . . is that really you? Am I hallucinating?" Chokha cried, his voice choking with tears. Vithoba walked through the doors, out of the temple to greet Chokha and hugged him. Leading him by his hand, Vithoba took Chokha into the temple.'

'A miracle!' exclaimed little Narayan.

'Yes indeed!' replied Sane Guruji.

'But surely it can't be true!' remarked Vishnu, whose rational mind could not make sense of miracles and magic. 'Surely, it's only a story.'

'Let me finish and then you can make up your mind,' Guruji advised.

'Chokha spent the night inside the temple, enjoying every moment with the Lord he had thirsted to meet. Vithoba playfully removed the garland from around his neck and put it around Chokha as a token of his love. It was finally morning and time for the temple gates to open. Vithoba led Chokha towards the door and bid him farewell.'

'This is unbelievable,' said Aruna. 'How can a stone idol talk to a person?'

Sane Guruji laughed. 'Your mother is far away in her village. Yet, do you not feel that you can connect with her? Vithu is a stone idol . . . yet, do you not have the faith that he will cure your Aai?'

Aruna did not quite understand what Guruji meant, but she nodded along.

'What happened then?'

'Early the next day, Chokha, delighted and delirious, ran out of the temple and made his way to the nearby river. When the priest entered the temple that morning, he saw that the garland around Vithoba was missing. But nobody could have entered the locked temple at night. Puzzled, he went out to search. And on the other side of the river, he noticed Chokha happily singing to himself with Vithoba's garland around his neck. The priest was furious and went charging towards Chokha.'

'Poor Chokhoba! They must have thought that he had stolen the garland!' Vishnu remarked.

'Yes! That's what they thought. As the priest neared Chokha, he noticed him sitting by the riverbank, eating lunch with his wife and chatting with an imaginary friend whom he called Vithu. Chokha could see him. But the priest couldn't. Chokha was offering Vithoba some curd to eat and they were chatting away.

'How dare this Mahar wear the garland of the lord around his neck and pretend to be chatting and eating with him!' the priest thundered. He marched towards the riverbank and slapped Chokha, admonishing him for his audacity. Chokha stood by with his head bowed low, holding on to his bruised cheek, humiliated but calm. The priest then took a dip in the river to purify himself for having touched Chokha and rushed back to the temple. Little did he know that he was in for a shock once he got there!'

'What? What happened at the temple?'

'When the priest stormed into the temple, feeling content for having punished Chokha, he stood before the idol of Vithal and almost fainted. The idol had a swollen cheek and curd spilt on its clothes!'

The gathering fell silent. The children looked on in amazement. The adults listened, slack-jawed.

'How did that happen?' demanded little Narayan.

'This is magic!' another child remarked

'This is impossible!' Vishnu exclaimed.

Guruji raised his hand. 'The priest realized something that day. He realized that Chokha was dear to Vithal, and that by insulting and hurting Chokha, he had insulted and hurt Lord Vithoba!' Sane Guruji explained.

'So . . . did he allow Chokha into the temple after that?' Aruna asked, praying for some magic, so she too could enter the temple.

Guruji shook his head. 'No . . . He was abolished from Pandharpur. Ordered to leave town immediately!'

Upon hearing this, Aruna was crestfallen.

'And yet . . . his faith remained steadfast. He did not give up or lose heart.'

'Guruji . . . why should we know the story of Chokha? Why narrate such a depressing story at this juncture?' an old man sitting at the back of the hall demanded.

'It may be depressing. But it is also inspiring. We are not the first ones to fight for equality, for our right to enter the Pandharpur Temple. Many great saints have walked this path before us. Let us, like Chokhoba, wear a smile upon our lips and persevere. Perhaps, the success that he could not taste might one day be ours.'

Aruna marvelled at the depth of Chokhoba's love for Vithal. He had endured curses and beatings and yet, hadn't lost his faith. And ultimately, he had found his Lord.

'Hundreds of years ago, they did not let Chokhoba enter the temple,' Sane Guruji said, holding up his hand. And then looking at Aruna, he added, 'But that was the past. You are the future. Don't let them stop you!'

4

BATTLEGROUND

'*Nahi Khulega Vithal Dwar, Sane Jao Bhima Paar!*'
Vithal's doors shall not be opened; Sane, go across the Bhima River!

'Nahi Khulega Vithal Dwar, Sane Jao Bhima Paar!'

'Nahi Khulega Vithal Dwar, Sane Jao Bhima Paar!'

The loud slogans caused Aruna to wake up with a start.

'Nahi Khulega Vithal Dwar, Sane Jao Bhima Paar!' The voices were growing louder.

Aruna ran to the window, where her brothers and some others stood transfixed, watching the spectacle. Pushing her way to the front, Aruna was shocked to find hundreds of people marching outside. They carried banners in their hands and were raising angry slogans.

'What's happened?' she gasped.

'Nahi Khulega Vithal Dwar, Sane Jao Bhima Paar!' the multitude screamed louder now as the mob neared the hall inside which Sane Guruji was resting.

'What . . . what is going on?' Aruna looked at her brothers, wide-eyed and scared.

'Can't you *see*?' whispered Vishnu, 'They want Sane Guruji to be sent away, just like Chokhoba! So that the temple can remain shut to us forever!'

'How can people be so heartless . . .' another boy cried openly. 'What have we ever done to them except be respectful—'

'Even the Shankaracharya supports our stance," a booming voice interrupted the little boy, referring to the revered head of the Shankara mutt. The loud voice seemed to be coming from a loudspeaker set up on a little makeshift stage in the maidan across the street.

'The Administrator of the Temple—that's him,' said Vishnu, through clenched teeth.

'Look, our brothers,' the voice boomed again, 'Priests and pontiffs from leading temples all across India have sent us letters of support! See!' he screamed, waving a sheaf of papers in his hand. 'Sane Guruji is wrong. He has no business meddling in things that have been the way they are for ages. That which is prescribed by our scriptures; our way of life. He must stop his protest at once! The temple cannot be opened to the low-borns. EVER!' he thundered.

'Nahi Khulega Vithal Dwar, Sane Jao Bhima Paar!' the crowds chanted endlessly, to the rhythm of a drumbeat.

Suddenly, a loudspeaker cackled from a platform at the other end of the maidan. Acharya Atre, one of the leaders supporting Sane Guruji, took the mike. 'Listen, my friends. Unless you allow Dalits to enter the temple, you have no right to enter the temple of freedom. The road to freedom passes *through* the temple,' Acharya Atre spoke with gusto. 'Untouchability and freedom can never go together. If we continue this evil practice, we shall insult our freedom fighters. I appeal to each one of you to allow the temple doors to be opened!'

A jeer rang aloud in the gathered crowd. 'Nahi Khulega Vithal Dwar, Sane Jao Bhima Paar!' The voices of those opposing entry into the temple for Dalits grew louder and more determined. People clapped along as the air echoed with slogans. They would not back down.

'Nahi Khulega Vithal Dwar, Sane Jao Bhima Paar!'

'May I remind you of the words of our great leader Dr Babasaheb Ambedkar,' Acharya Atre continued, as if he hadn't heard the crowds. 'If over 50 million people are to live in captivity after India becomes free, is that freedom not meaningless? As we stand at the threshold of freedom, how would we answer those who died for our Independence? We must act. Let's open our temples, open our wells and open our hearts!' he implored.

Loud cheers went up amongst those in the hall and the crowds that had gathered outside. Yet, the stirring speech had no impact on those on the other side.

'This man is talking nonsense!' the priest bellowed from the podium on the other side. 'Our *shastras* do not permit this. Our scriptures do not permit this. It is sacrilege! We will invite the wrath of the gods!' a member of the priestly community raised a clamour from the other end.

'Nahi Khulega Vithal Dwar, Sane Jao Bhima Paar!' The noise of the drums was deafening.

From the other side of the ground another dissenting voice now rang out. 'We stand upon the holy earth of Pandharpur! Where the great saints of Maharashtra have tread . . . Let not the wisdom of Sant Dnyaneshwar and Eknath, the glories of Sant

Namdev and Tukaram, go to waste! Let us rise to be deserving of their legacy.'

'Why do you endure curses?' said another, reading out a message written by Ambedkar. 'Chokha went into the temple resolutely. You are the descendants of Chokha. Why do you fear to enter the temple? Brace yourself like a wrestler. Come . . . together, let us conquer these misconceived ideas of pollution!'

'Even Lord Rama had to abide by this dharma!' the man at the other end retorted. 'And so, the Varnashrama dharma cannot be overturned. Caste and pollution rules cannot be questioned. Who are *these* people to challenge the law of dharma?'

'Jai Shree Rama!' the crowds bellowed.

'There will be disaster. Do not anger the gods!' the speaker continued. 'There will be drought and famine. Disease and death. Misery and misfortune! The skies will rain blood. Babies will be born deformed. There will be hunger and helplessness all around. Mark my words. Do not challenge the shastras. The world will end. There will be a pralaya!' he finished his tirade with a prophecy of an apocalypse.

'Tai . . . Tai . . . is that trrrrue?' stuttered little Narayan, turning to Aruna 'If we are allowed into the temple, will the world come to an end?'

'Don't be foolish! These are all excuses!' Vishnu said, brushing his younger brother aside. 'These are just ploys . . . They put fear into people's minds so they won't question and protest! Don't you believe them!'

Aruna wanted to believe her older brother but she wasn't quite as sure as him. Surely, she did not want to risk bringing about the end of the world! Seeing fear and uncertainty in her eyes, Vishnu pulled her pigtails. 'Silly girl!' he laughed. 'Back in the village you climb the tallest trees and swim in the deepest wells without any fear! And here, you are scared of empty threats! Crooked truths, all of them!'

'Gurujiiiiiiiiii!' a loud cry was suddenly heard across the hall. The children turned around to see a group of people running towards Sane Guruji. The old leader was lying motionless upon a mat in the front of the hall.

'What happened? What happened to Guruji?' asked a lady, anxiously.

'His pulse is falling!' replied the young bespectacled boy who had sent Sane Guruji's telegram to Gandhiji the previous day.

'Pulse . . . What does that mean?' Aruna asked Vishnu, panting as they rushed to Guruji's side.

'It means his health is not looking good,' Vishnu replied.

'He hasn't eaten for ten days!' the lady sitting beside Guruji said. 'We must get him to drink some lemon juice at least.'

'He is not responding!' cried the bespectacled boy, tears streaming down his cheeks. 'Guruji . . . Guruji please get up and eat something. *Please*,' he wept.

An older man hurried towards the front. He held on to Guruji's arm and felt his pulse. Pulling out a stethoscope, he examined his chest.

'Doctor . . . please tell us Guruji is all right!' pleaded the lady.

'He is not looking good,' the doctor replied, looking tense. 'We must get something into his system. He is old and this fast has taken a toll on him.'

'But he won't listen!' the youth cried.

'Nahi Khulega Vithal Dwar, Sane Jao Bhima Paar!' the noise outside was bursting through the walls. Loudspeakers blared.

People screamed. Leaders continued their stirring speeches and the crowds continued raising angry slogans. The young boy hurriedly closed the windows to keep out the chaos. An old woman sat in a corner, anxiously reciting verses from the Gita. Two others ran about, carrying messages about Guruji's condition to the people enquiring outside. The doctor sat nervously by his side, monitoring his condition.

Aruna's eyes were glued to Sane Guruji, watching his chest heave up and down with every gentle breath he took. The hubbub inside the hall and the chaos outside of it blurred out of her focus. Her attention was only on Guruji, on his every breath. In him, she had seen hope that her mother would be cured. And now the beacon of her hope was fading.

Grey clouds gathered in the sky and the room was swallowed by darkness. Lightning struck and the heavens roared. The howling wind threw open the latched windows. The crowds ran helter-skelter to find shelter. And then, as if to wash away the madness at Pandharpur with its fury, the rain tore through the rumbling skies. The speeches ended, the loudspeakers went off, the slogans stopped and the crowds disappeared.

Inside the hall, the darkness brought with it an overbearing sense of gloom. Aruna closed her eyes and saw her mother's smiling face. Sensed her warm presence. And then, suddenly, she could see the face no more. It disappeared into a black abyss of darkness. Aruna sunk her head into her little palms and began to weep.

5

LIBERATION

'The temple will be opened to all! The temple will be opened to all!' cried two young boys, as they rushed into the hall, waving newspapers in their hands.

'The law has been passed! Temples will be open to all!'

After a stunned silence, a wave of excitement surged through the quiet hall. The first rays of dawn had brought along hope with light. People stood up and crowded around the two young messengers, hardly able to believe the news they bore.

'Guruji . . . Guruji, did you hear?' the two boys dashed towards Sane Guruji. "We have won! Our prayers have been heard! The Pandharpur Temple is to be open to everybody! A law has been passed making it everybody's right! Nobody can be denied entry into temples!'

All eyes turned towards Guruji. He was motionless.

'Guruji . . . Guruji . . .' the young bespectacled boy whispered, bending low and speaking into his ears. 'The Temple will be opened to all! Your fast has been successful!'

Could he hear? Or was he too weak to register what was going on? Guruji did not move. Everyone waited with bated breath. The boy repeated the good news a little louder, shaking Guruji gently by his shoulders. The anxious crowd looked on. But Guruji did not stir.

Tears filled Aruna's eyes as she feared the worst. Her last memory from the night returned. She saw the cold icy hands of death taking a monstrous grip over her mother and snatching her further and further away, disappearing into an unending abyss of darkness. She saw Sane Guruji's smiling face which was also fast disappearing into the dark pit. 'Oh Vithu!' Aruna cried aloud, 'I came here trusting you. Don't let me down!'

'Quick!' said the doctor, who had been monitoring Guruji through the night, to the boy. 'Go and get some *moong-pani* to break his fast. He must eat!'

Half a dozen people rushed towards the back of the hall to get things ready. Another group began chanting Vithoba's name, praying for their leader.

'At this old age and in this heat, Guruji has gone without food for ten whole days . . . So that we may enjoy our rights. So that we are treated with dignity, like . . . humans. This is a story that must be told!' a young lady told the children. 'Go back to your villages and homes and tell your people. When you grow up . . . tell your children and grandchildren . . . so they will remember the *price* of this freedom. You have seen history being created here!'

Aruna nodded. She would ensure this story would not be forgotten.

'Guruji . . . please allow me to feed you some moong-pani,' pleaded the bespectacled boy, with a bowl in hand. 'We have won! The temple will be opened to all! Your fast has succeeded.'

Still, Guruji did not move.

'You know . . . Guruji loves children,' interjected the young lady. 'Why don't you ask the little girl to try?' she suggested, pushing Aruna ahead.

Aruna willingly took the bowl and approached Guruji with trembling hands. Her eyes were brimming with tears. 'Thank you, Guruji,' she whispered in his ears. 'Because of your fast, I can enter the temple and meet Vithoba and ask him to make Aai all right again. The temple is now going to be open to everybody.'

The old man turned his head ever so slightly towards the child's voice and his lips parted in a subtle smile. The people standing around were moved to tears.

'Please Guruji, eat something now. We can't wait to go to the temple, but we want to hold your hand as we go in.'

Guruji nodded to acknowledge that he had heard and followed. He did not have the strength to reply with words, but the crowd cheered; their beloved leader was going to be all right.

Two men moved closer and propped up Sane Guruji's shoulders upon their lap. The lady held the spoon in Aruna's hands and slowly guided the moong-pani towards his parched lips. As he sipped slowly, a sense of jubilation ran through the hall. People hugged each other and wept.

They had pulled off a historic victory.

'Bala . . . the temple shall now be open to all! You can see your Vithoba and ask him to cure Aai!' Aruna's Baba said, throwing his arms around his three children. The long-drawn battle and the years of humiliation were finally over. Aruna smiled half-heartedly. She couldn't wait to go into the temple. But there was one worry that still nagged her.

'But Baba . . . is Vithu still divine? The bhatji said they had washed away his divinity. Can Vithu still cure Aai?' Aruna asked her father, deep furrows of worry crowding her little forehead.

'Bala . . . it is your *faith* that makes Vithoba divine!' Tuka replied. 'How could anyone wash that away?'

Hearing her father's reply, Aruna's face lit up. 'Vithoba, here I come!' she proclaimed joyfully. 'I'm certain you will help Aai!'

The faith and innocence in his daughter's eyes moved Tuka to tears. India was changing. Freedom—real freedom—something he had never enjoyed, was perhaps finally within his children's grasp.

At the far end of the hall, a group began singing, to celebrate the joyous moment. The soulful words of Chokhoba rang through the air.

'Cane is crooked. But its juice is not,
Why be fooled by outward appearance?
The bow is crooked but the arrow is not,
Why be fooled by outward appearance?
The river is twisting, but its water is not,
Why be fooled by outward appearance?
Chokha may be ugly but his feelings are not,
Why be fooled by outward appearance?'

Aruna closed her eyes and sang along. She did not fear climbing the tallest trees. She did not fear jumping into the deepest wells. She would not fear crooked truths!

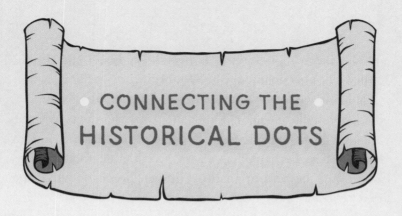

CONNECTING THE HISTORICAL DOTS

 ## UNDERSTANDING HIERARCHY

It has been commonplace, since time immemorial, for human beings to classify everything they know into categories. Often, this is done to understand complex phenomena by putting a large number of objects in some order. For instance, the vast plant kingdom is classified into various categories such as grasses, trees, herbs, shrubs and so on. This is done on the basis of qualities such as size, appearance, etc. However, such classifications do not lead to hierarchies or orders in which one is regarded as superior to another. So, grasses are not seen as being superior to shrubs. They are just different: differentiation without discrimination.

There is another kind of classification, which does not result from inherent qualities but instead from notions that are artificially constructed and imposed. For example, the idea of race, the notion of royalty, the notion of normalcy. The king is regarded as being special and different from his subjects. For a long time, white-skinned people were regarded as being superior to those with brown or black skin. Such classifications and notions of superiority arise from ideas *created* by humans. Differentiation leading to discrimination.

You too occupy a place in some form of social hierarchy, whether you like it or not. Think about your home, your family, your classroom, your society. Is there a noticeable hierarchy? Look harder. Perhaps you are so accustomed to it that you cannot look beyond it. In many Indian homes, boys or men are regarded as more important than girls or women. In several classrooms, those that perform well in maths and science are regarded as more intelligent than those who are good at art or sports. Those with fair skin are considered more beautiful than those who have a dark complexion. A rich man stepping out of a Mercedes is considered more important than a soot-covered mason laying bricks at a construction site. A child who is deaf or one who stammers while speaking is somehow considered inferior or abnormal.

What do you think of this hierarchy? Do you, like Aruna's father, accept the hierarchy that has been imposed upon you? Or do you, like Sane Guruji and Aruna, question the basis of such discrimination?

Caste is one form of social hierarchy. Gender is another basis for creating a hierarchy. For centuries in India, certain people have been seen as 'polluting' or 'dirtying' factors. They have been considered impure due to their birth, profession or gender. Such an order in society has been justified or made to be seen as correct on the basis of scriptures or custom. Starting from the 7th century in South India, a movement known as the Bhakti Movement led to a social upheaval across the country where discrimination was questioned by social reformers and saints. Women and people of lower castes began to find their voice.

Everywhere in the world, when discrimination has led to oppression, the oppressed have revolted to overthrow this human-imposed hierarchy. The French Revolution, the Russian Revolution and the American Civil War are instances of other such movements that were born out of hierarchy, discrimination and oppression. Perhaps, you can find out more about these movements and trace their impact on your own life.

There may be several social structures that we overlook because things have always been that way. And when you think hard about it, they might seem oppressive. Can you identify some of those?

Start with making a list of various social orders in which you occupy a place. What is the hierarchy of that order? How do you imagine Aruna felt when she was brushed aside rudely merely because she was born into another caste? Can you think of a social order without a hierarchy? Or do you think hierarchy is a natural outcome when two groups are perceived as being different?

UNBOX THE PAST: FIND HISTORY HIDDEN IN THIS STORY.

 CHOKHA

Chokhamela or Chokhoba was a 14th century poet-saint of western India and belonged to what is known as the Varkari tradition of Maharashtra. The Varkaris are devotees of Vithal, lovingly known as Vithoba, widely regarded as Lord Krishna.

Chokhoba belonged to the Mahar caste, a group deemed untouchables or dalits. He was looked down upon and severely ill-treated because of his caste; he was never allowed to enter the temple of Vithal at Pandharpur, outside which he stood for days because he was born into a 'lower-caste'.

Along with Tiruppan Alvar and Nandanar (Tamil saint-poets, circa AD 8), Chokhoba is one of the early Dalit poets of India.

BHAKTI MOVEMENT

The Bhakti movement began in South India in about the 7th century and gradually became a pan-Indian movement. It led to people questioning the old traditions, biases and religious practices. The Bhakti saints focussed on devotion as a means of achieving proximity to God and that resulted in people across society, including women and those from the lower castes, participating in religion and society.

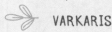 VARKARIS

Each year, in the month of August, thousands of Varkaris begin a pilgrimage to the town of Pandharpur in Maharashtra. Forming groups known as *dindis*, they start from various towns carrying a palki or palanquin, containing footprints of saint-poets, singing abhangs or devotional hymns.

Dnyaneshwar is one of the first Varkari saints. Some other names you may have heard of are Namdev, Eknath, Janabai and Tukaram. A number of Varkari poets like Savta Mali, Gora Kumbhar and Chokhamela belonged to lower castes. Their abhangs are sung and performed with great fervour to this day.

 GOD IN A COPPER POT

The shocking event narrated in the story, where the idol of Vithal is washed and water is collected in a copper vessel, actually did take place in Pandharpur in May 1947, at the threshold of India's independence.

Mantras were recited by the temple priests, to remove the shadow of people from the 'lower castes' and to save the divine nature of the deity. The copper pot containing the supposed divinity of Vithoba was then taken by one of the priests to his own house and prayers were offered to the pot!

It is said that years later, a cat happened to pounce on the pot and much to the horror of the believers; the supposedly divine waters were washed away!

 ## SANE GURUJI

Pandurang Sane (popularly known as Sane Guruji) was a political worker, social reformer and a writer of children's stories. Born in 1899 in Maharashtra, he was moved by the plight of the Dalits as they were not treated as humans and denied basic rights. So, he launched a movement demanding that Dalits be permitted entry into temples. As a result, several temples opened their doors. The priests of the Vithoba temple at Pandharpur, however, refused. Following that, Sane Guruji undertook a fast to urge the temple authorities to relent. The fast and the enactment of the law that followed are real and significant historical events.

THE SWEEPER OF BAREILLY

1

A WRETCHED LIFE

'Don't you wish you could do something other than clean people's shit?' Mori asked Sukha, as they sat on their haunches, clearing another pile of night soil from behind the village headman's home.

Sukha didn't react. Mori was young and would learn the realities of their life soon enough. Their destiny as sweepers was decided before their birth. They were *born* sweepers. Born to *be* sweepers. Disposing of dead animals, clearing human excreta and sweeping the streets was designated as their lot in life—long before they'd drawn their first breath. *Why question these things when there was no escape?* he thought to himself.

'Sukha, you wretched creature! Don't sit around whiling away your time!' screamed the village headman, from a window in the house. 'Go and clean the courtyard immediately! I'm expecting guests!'

'*Ji* sahib,' Sukha mumbled, his head bent low, as he hurried onward to the courtyard with his broom. In large brisk strokes, Sukha swept the dust and fallen leaves from the yard as Mori slowly gathered them all into a basket with his little hands.

'Quick now,' whispered Sukha worriedly, 'Hurry up!' The sahib's guests were approaching. Sukha recognized one of them as the village postmaster. Who the other man was, Sukha couldn't tell. Either way, there was no time to wait and find out. Sukha and Mori could not be seen when the guests arrived. Their presence would pollute them, make them dirty.

But it was too late!

'You have defiled me with your shadow!' the postmaster and his friend stepped back in disgust, as they spotted the boy in the courtyard.

Mori scurried out of the courtyard behind Sukha.

'Please excuse him, sir,' Sukha mumbled, keeping a distance from the sahibs and his head bent, as was the norm. 'He is only a child and has yet to learn! I am deeply sorry, sir! Please excuse him.'

'Good heavens!' the post-master muttered. 'Now I shall have to go and take a dip in the river again.'

'Bugger off! Bugger off!' the village headman emerged from his home with a copper jar in his hand. 'I told the brute to clean the courtyard hours ago! But these lazy donkeys don't work! And then they come and pollute us!' Sprinkling water from the jar on his visitors, he invited his guests inside.

'Forget those filthy creatures! We have more important news,' whispered the post master's friend, as they walked into the courtyard towards the house. 'There is news that a war has broken out.'

Standing at a distance, Sukha's ears pricked up.

'Really? Where?' asked the village headman in alarm, still in the courtyard.

'In Europe. Between the Germans and the British.'

'Hahaha! And why is that of any concern to us in Bareilly?' the headman laughed.

'Of course it is, my friend! The British are recruiting Indian soldiers,' the Postmaster continued. 'And I heard that they're willing to pay well.'

Still standing at a safe distance, Sukha straightened himself and looked thoughtfully at Mori. The question the child had asked him only minutes ago, came back to him. Of course he wished he could do something other than clean people's shit and dirt. *But what was this now? A war had broken out somewhere and the Angrez were recruiting Indians!* Sukha's eyes lit up.

Above him, dark clouds were approaching from the west. The monsoon would soon be here. The long dusty summer was finally coming to an end. And with it, Sukha reckoned, maybe his destiny might change. *Maybe,* he mused.

Perhaps, Sukha imagined for the first time in his life, there was going to be an escape from this wretched life after all!

2

SAILING IN HOPE

Clutching the brown satchel nervously in his hand, Sukha took a deep breath, soaking in the sea breeze that gently caressed his face. He had never seen the sea before. It was . . . marvellous! Limitless. Boundless.

Staring into the vastness, amused by the gulls that circled above them, Sukha felt a surge of hope. That life at the other side, wherever that may be, would offer him a better deal.

'Come along, come on board!' a tall English sahib ushered the group in, as Sukha followed the others over the little draw bridge into the large ship that was to be his home for the next few weeks. Sukha didn't understand a word of English. He didn't need to. His job was to scrub the ship and keep it clean. A job he knew only too well. And for which he found good company in his co-sweeper Ganya.

'It is so exciting to be going to *vilayat*!' Ganya exclaimed to Sukha, with a twinkle in his eye, as they got down to scrubbing the ship's floors. "I've heard they have funny toilets there!' he chuckled. 'And that they don't use water after they finish up!'

Intrigued as Sukha was, he couldn't help laughing. From the prospect of freedom to the shape of the toilets, everything about these foreign lands seemed fascinating.

In a few days, the ship was ready and Sukha watched wide-eyed as soldiers boarded in their crisp khaki uniforms, carrying bundles of luggage. Broad-shouldered Sardars. Towering Jats. Fierce-looking Gurkhas. Fair-skinned Garhwalis. Indian soldiers from everywhere poured in. Dozens of Rajas and Nawabs across India had pledged their armies to fight shoulder to shoulder with the British.

Sukha couldn't help noticing the great fellowship on board. British officers chatted merrily with Indian jawans, high-caste Jats who never mingled with low-caste workers back in the village, sang songs and played games like they were brothers.

'War can do strange things!' remarked Gangaram, the *beeshti* who, like Sukha, had come all the way from Bareilly to serve as water-man. 'Nothing brings rivals together like a common enemy does!'

'What about you? What brings you here Sardarji?' asked Gangaram, of Subedar Mandeep Singh, a tall soldier from Punjab, who was seated next to them. 'Why are you prepared to lay down your life for the firangis?'

'Well, the money is better than what I get back at home,' the Sardar replied, twirling his moustache. 'And besides, never again will I get a chance to go on this kind of an adventure!'

'Hmmm . . . frankly, that's what brought me here too,' responded Shahnawaz Hussain, a fierce-looking soldier. 'When will I ever get a chance to see pardes if I don't grab this opportunity?'

On good days, Sukha listened to these conversations after he had finished clearing the mules' and horses' dung below deck and scrubbed the salt residue from the ocean spray off the decks. A part of him agreed. The prospect of adventure excited him as well. Moreover, he had on him a pair of clean clothes, received three meals each day and was in the service of His Majesty. What more could he want?

On bad days, Sukha clutched his retching stomach and regretted his decision to sign up for the services. As the ship pitched and tossed on the high seas and the roaring of the winds and buffeting of the waves were the only sounds that fell on his ear, Sukha cursed himself for aspiring for a better life.

And in those moments, Sukha looked heavenward and wondered, like each one of the thousands of Indian soldiers headed to the battlefront, whether he'd ever get to see his home again.

3

UNKNOWN SHORES

'You are the descendants of men who have been great rulers and warriors!' a message from King George was read out to the Indian troops as they disembarked at Marseilles in France. 'You will recall the glories of your race, you will have the honour of showing in Europe, that the sons of India have lost none of their ancient martial instincts. History will record the doings of India's sons and your children will proudly tell of the deeds of their fathers!'

'Jo Bole So Nihal, Sat Sri Akal!' a Sikh solder raised the slogan and the entire battalion reverberated with the war cry in acknowledgment.

Sukha looked around puzzled, as a loud cheer from the troops greeted the announcement.

'The king of England has sent us a message!' Subedar Mandeep Singh explained to Sukha and the others who couldn't follow English. 'The king himself!'

Sukha's shoulders broadened. Ganya stood straight with his chin up and head high. Gangaram smiled as his chest swelled with pride. The king had sent them a message! The king himself! They had never felt so important before.

'Indienne! Indienne!' French women waved out as the contingent marched on the roads. The streets were swarming with locals, every footpath was lined with crowds, people were craning their necks out of balconies, standing glued to window panes of cafes, to catch a glimpse of the Indian soldiers who had travelled miles from the exotic east to help them fight their war.

'Look at those babies with such rosy cheeks!' Gangaram chuckled, staring at the children flanking the streets, curious to get a glimpse at the brown-skinned Indians.

'And look at these women with golden hair! Their skin is so white!' Ganya laughed, gawking at the blonde women excitedly waving and cheering for the soldiers.

'Oh! Look . . . that woman even kissed Singh sahib on his cheek!' exclaimed Gangaram, clapping his hands and laughing like a child.

As they travelled through city and town, pasture and countryside, the roar of the crowds and the waving flags delighted Sukha. He gradually began to smile back awkwardly in acknowledgment, still unsure about how to react to all the respect. No one had ever welcomed him so joyfully before. Sukha was filled with pride.

'Look!' Gangaram tugged at Sukha's arm as they craned their necks out of the window of the train taking them to Orleans, 'That's an airplane! Look how it flies like an eagle!'

Sukha turned his neck up through the window and watched in awe as the monstrous bird of metal glided above their heads, making a giant whirring sound. 'Now, where would I have seen such things sitting in my little village in Bareilly?' Gangaram exclaimed, wiping his tears, overwhelmed. 'This is the magic of vilayat!'

'Yes! If only I didn't have to suffer this horrible thing they call teacake!' Subedar Mandeep Singh sighed. 'How awful it tastes! Can we not get some ghee-laden ladoos here?'

'And some masala milk!' laughed Shahnawaz Hussain, 'With some hot *malpua!*'

As the train hurtled towards the battleground, soldiers laughed and reminisced about their home. Musings turned into conversations and conversations into songs. The French countryside reverberated with Indian songs of love for the people they had left behind in a land far away.

Sukha smiled. The music lifted his spirits as he watched the smoke of the engine billowing in the wind. He was going to fight a war. And yet, strangely, he was happy. Nobody had called him *wretched dog* or *wicked scoundrel* for weeks. Nor did he have to run or hide to keep his shadow from polluting the village chief. His mornings didn't begin with cleaning other people's shit.

Sukha was having the best time of his life!

4

FIGHTING FOR WHOM?

Nothing prepared Sukha for the moment Gangaram's brains splattered on his face.

'Ganga! Ganga!' Sukha cried out in horror, holding the dead weight of his friend in his arms, pulling him back into the trenches. 'Help! Help! Help!' he shouted, looking around in desperation. His head swam. The wounded were calling out for help from every direction, their voices drowned out every few seconds by the booming guns. Heavy smoke clouded their vision.

Sukha placed Gangaram's limp body down on the floor and checked for signs of breathing. None. He checked for a pulse. Nothing. A bullet had gone straight through Gangaram's head. The beeshti, still carrying a camel-skin satchel on his shoulders, had died serving water to soldiers in a war that was not his own.

Sitting on his haunches, Sukha stared disbelievingly into Gangaram's lifeless eyes. *He was always full of laughter,* he thought, as tears rolled down his cheeks.

'I don't understand why these white people are fighting other white people!' Gangaram had quipped only a few days ago. 'They all worship the same God! They all read the same Holy Book! They all celebrate the same festivals! What on earth are they fighting over? And why are *we* fighting *for* them?'

Sukha had not understood either. *What was the war all about?* It had seemed a blur and now even more so.

Why were they fighting? For whom? What for?

The questions, which had troubled the mighty warrior Arjuna on the battlefield of Kurukshetra in the legends that Sukha had heard, came back to him amidst the whir of bullets and the blast of grenades, as a blanket of smoke rose above the dead and the dying.

'Subedar Mandeep Singh has been hurt! Go help him!' a sharp voice cut into his thoughts.

Sukha whirred around, looking for the man. Subedar Mandeep Singh had been standing beside him less than two minutes ago! He had rushed out of the trenches with a wheelbarrow to help an English captain who had taken a hit in the heavy firing.

Sukha's vision was blurred with hot tears. Men from Jalandar and Bareilly were laying down their lives for people from England and France. To defend the lives and freedom of the very people who had ruled them and robbed them of their own independence! It suddenly seemed so senseless.

'Quick Sukha!' he heard a voice from somewhere. 'Clear up the bodies! Now!'

Still looking at the dead face of Gangaram, Sukha straightened up. There was no time to grieve or mourn.

He had a job to do. To clear out the piles of dead bodies from the trenches so that another batch of soldiers could fill in and prepare to die.

A retching sensation took over him. It had been six months since they had left home. All around him, cannons boomed. Machine guns fired. The smoke from the gunfire, the sound of the grenade blasts, the moans of wounded men grappling with death. Corpses at every step. Streams of blood and rainwater flowing through little channels in the ground. It seemed as though the whole world would come to an end.

And the icy winds blowing in from the north did nothing to alleviate his suffering. The cold was freezing his bones. The sun hardly made an appearance. The ground was covered in a layer of snow. Sukha and all the Indian soldiers, ill-prepared in their thin cotton khakis, for the wind, sleet and rain of the European winter, shivered and trembled. Just the week before, Ganya had died of frostbite.

The long johns and coats that had been sent for them by the British did not fit. They were too large. The blankets too few. The dampness and the cold seeped through the thin layers and entered his bones. Yet there was no time to brood or rest. There was a job to be done.

The wonders of vilayat had long ceased.

Sukha yearned for peace. Sukha wished to return home. Sukha prayed for escape: from one hell, back to another.

5

A WRETCHED END

Sukha looked up at the skies in gratitude when the orders were translated for him. 'The number of injured soldiers has gone up. We need more hands at the hospital. Sukha, you shall report to the hospital at England and join duties there as a latrine cleaner.'

Sukha's game of hide-and-seek was over. He had lost. Fate had won.

He was to be, once more, a sweeper.

But Sukha was also relieved. Glad to get away from the guns. And as he arrived at his new posting in England, it didn't seem like a bad deal to him at all.

The hospital was warm and furnished with rugs and carpets. Music from the gramophone played light peppy music to keep patients in good spirits. The special kitchen served Indian food. There were wide bright corridors with open lawns. Copies of the Bhagwad Gita, the Guru Granth Sahib and the Koran were being flown in to ease the suffering of the wounded soldiers. It was no paradise but at least, Sukha reckoned, he didn't live every moment wondering if it was going to be his last.

'I don't feel quite so well,' Sukha felt like saying to his superintendent each morning. But he didn't. There was much work to be done. The floors had to be scraped and the toilets had to be cleaned. Besides, he didn't want them to think he was a shirker. And given the grim scene all around him, Sukha didn't feel it was right to complain at all.

'Oh, why has Wahe Guru kept me alive?' a soldier who had lost his eyesight in battle, kept repeating to others in the ward. 'This life is a curse!'

'What will I do after I return home? How will I work the plough in my fields without my hands?' wept another, over his lost limbs.

There was no time for Sukha to waste. Those around him were missing limbs. Some had lost their eyes. Still others were without fingers or toes, frostbitten. Patients howled in pain, cursed in agony, cried out for a last look at their parents and wives and children back home. Sukha felt he ought not to complain about his own pain, which didn't seem half as bad. Ignoring his condition, Sukha continued to serve. In his own silent way, he tried also to comfort those in pain, offering them a patient ear, a gentle nod in their most trying moments. Nobody noticed him. Nobody knew his name. After all, he was *just* the cleaner.

'The moon . . .' cried out Subedar Mandeep Singh one night, looking out through his window at the silvery ball in the sky. 'The same moon I see up there is shining down on my children back home in Jalandar!' he sighed. 'How fortunate she is! If only god would give me one last chance to see their smiling faces again!'

Sukha listened in silence and wiped his own tears. He too missed Mori, his innocent toothless smile flashing every day before his teary eyes. He wished he could hold his son near and tell him all about his adventures and experiences. Sukha wished for Mori to know that his father had tried. Tried to battle with his fate. Tried so Mori could have a better life.

The cold was getting more bitter now in this foreign land and the pain in Sukha's lungs grew sharper. His vision went blurry often. Sometimes, he'd experience a blackout and collapse. He yearned for some rest. And for the warm sun on his back. But he didn't hold out any hope that it might actually happen. Life had never been kind enough to grant him any wishes.

The king wrote to them once again to raise their spirits. His message was read out. 'Well done, you soldiers of India! You have come here and rendered me great assistance. You will recover and do your duty well again!'

But this time, neither Subedar Mandeep Singh nor Sukha would feel elated to hear the king's message.

Mandeep Singh's body was cold, limp and still.

Sukha's lay in a lifeless heap.

A gangrene infection had robbed the life of the brave soldier who had selflessly dashed into the line of fire to help an Englishman.

The cold hands of pneumonia consumed Sukha, who had been scrubbing toilet floors till his last day.

Subedar Mandeep Singh's body was taken to the Sikh crematorium for cremation with honours.

Sukha's body stayed in the morgue.

It was a good thing the dead don't hear, that Sukha couldn't hear what was being said about him.

'He is an untouchable,' the Pundit told the authorities, after examining his records. 'We cannot cremate him here in the Hindu crematorium.'

'He is not a Muslim,' the Maulvi pointed out after perusing the facts. 'We cannot bury him in the cemetery.'

'But,' argued the hospital administrator, 'He was Indian. What would you have us do with his body?'

'It is not our concern,' said the cleric with a shrug. 'In order to be buried in the cemetery, he must be a Muslim—which he is not.'

'I agree,' the Pundit nodded. 'And nor is he a caste Hindu. He cannot be cremated at our crematorium.'

There was no escape for Sukha in life.

There would be no escape for Sukha in death.

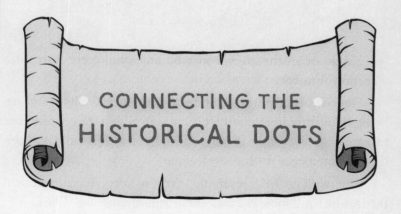

CONNECTING THE
HISTORICAL DOTS

 AFFIRMATIVE ACTION

The story of Sukha, sad and shocking as it is, is based on true events. Oppressed and disadvantaged, Sukha was shunned in life, and in death, due to his caste.

Perhaps you have not encountered the phenomenon of caste discrimination in any significant way. But you may have noticed subtle signs of discrimination. For instance, have you noticed separate plates or glasses being used for domestic staff or workers? Have you tried to find out why?

Speaking to those who've grown up in smaller towns or villages will help you find out more about caste. Find out if back in their home town or village, they are able to sit together and eat with people from other castes. From separate wells for water to separate seating in schools, to stories of beatings and humiliation, you may hear many tales of horror. Can you imagine something like that in your school? How would you feel if you were made to sit separately or in the corner just because you were born into a certain family?

One way to fight this unfair treatment of fellow human beings is 'affirmative action'. It is a way in which the government takes specific measures to help a group of people who have been discriminated against for several years.

Reservation, i.e., reserving certain seats in educational institutions and jobs, is a form of affirmative action. The aim of this measure is to provide a level playing field and an opportunity for those who have suffered caste discrimination for centuries. It has been a topic of hot debates in India for decades.

Some say that reservation is for the benefit of those like Sukha, who had been kept out of the fold of learning, education and dignity for centuries, thus giving them a chance to climb out of the situation and live a life of respect and dignity.

However, some people claim that reservation is unfair as it ignores academic merit and achievement, and that it leads to those less deserving of it, to get seats in colleges and jobs in offices, while those who are more deserving are left behind. This, in turn, according to them, is resulting in a brain drain, with the best students going out of the country to pursue higher education and jobs.

This debate then boils down to the question of 'what is merit?' Is it the result of one's own actions alone? Or is it the accumulated benefit of generations of advantage and privilege? If a group of people have been humiliated and oppressed for centuries, such as Sukha was, is it not reasonable that they are extended some help in rising out of that condition?

Then, there is another layer to this debate. Some people think that while reservation is a good thing, it ought to have some limits. They feel that it must be extended only to people who are financially or economically backward. Others feel it is the social stigma that is more of a setback than the financial status and hence, reservation ought to be based on social criterion.

What do you think?

Reservation has been a raging debate in India ever since Independence and is likely to remain so for many years to come. Do you agree with affirmative action? If yes, what kinds of affirmative action would you extend to a group of disadvantaged people? Discuss this in your class or at home, with Sukha's story in mind.

UNBOX THE PAST: DISCOVER HISTORY HIDDEN IN THE STORY.

 WHY DID INDIAN SOLDIERS FIGHT FOR THE BRITISH?

World War I broke out in June 1914 between Great Britain, France, Russia and Japan on one side and Germany, Austria, Hungary and Turkey on the other. Later, Italy and USA also joined the war.

Initially, it appeared that India was far away from it all until the German ship Emden attacked Chennai (then Madras) on the night of 22 September 1914, which brought the war to India's shores.

Indian leaders believed that if India supported the British in the war, Britain would be grateful and pay India back in kind, by giving it more freedom.

Several Indian rulers and kings provided soldiers and other materials towards Britain's war effort. About a million Indian soldiers participated in the war in support of Great Britain. Tens of thousands of Indians were killed fighting for the British cause.

India did not, however, benefit from the help extended to Britain. The war led to higher prices, heavy taxation, food shortages and poverty.

BRITAIN'S GIFT FOR INDIA'S SUPPORT IN THE WAR: JALLIANWALA BAGH

Many soldiers who had sacrificed life and limb for the cause of the British in the World War I were Sikhs from Punjab. Far from gratitude and appreciation, their relatives were met with a brutal shock after the end of the war.

In March 1919, the British passed the Rowlatt Act, which authorized the government to imprison any person without trial in a court of law. This came as a sudden blow to the Indian leaders, who were expecting Britain to be more considerate towards India's demands for self-government.

Gandhiji asked people to disregard the act and court arrest. A great hartal was called on 6 April 1919. This was met with great support from the Indian people. Several leaders were arrested by the government, particularly in Punjab, as a part of this agitation.

On 13 April 1919, a crowd gathered to protest against the arrest of their leaders at Jallianwala Bagh in Amritsar, Punjab. The bagh was an open space enclosed on three sides by buildings, and contained only one exit.

General Dyer, the Military Commander of Amritsar, surrounded the bagh with his army unit and ordered his men to shoot with rifles and machine guns at unarmed civilians. General Dyer ordered his soldiers to continue firing until the last bullet was spent.

Several hundreds of innocent men, women and children were killed instantly in the massacre. Many died during the night as they could not be rescued due to the curfew imposed in the city. Thousands were injured. The massacre shook India.

This incident took place within just six months of the end of the war, where people like Sukha had laid down their lives for the British. Gandhi, who had supported the British war effort, became disillusioned with British rule. Rabindranath Tagore returned his Knighthood in protest. The Indian freedom struggle took on a new momentum.

Jallianwala Bagh was a bitter end to the help India had extended to Britain in the war. Many years later, when World War II broke out, Britain once again dragged India into the war. Once bitten, twice shy, Gandhi and the Indian leaders refused to cooperate with Britain's war effort. If Britain wanted India as an ally, the Congress told Britain, it must grant India complete independence. Britain refused. In response, Gandhiji launched the Quit India movement in 1942.

 ## THE END OF SUKHA

Sukha was finally laid to rest at St Nicholas' Church, Brockenhurst in England. When neither the Hindu crematorium nor the Islamic cemetery agreed to perform his last rites, the people of Brockenhurst decided to bury Sukha in the churchyard. Local parishioners of the church raised money for a headstone in the yard in his memory and the epitaph on it reads as follows:

'He left country, home and friends, to serve our King & Empire, in the Great European War . . . But his earthly life was sacrificed in the interests of others . . .'

INDIA GATE: A MEMORIAL

India Gate, standing in the heart of New Delhi, is a well-known landmark and symbol of our capital city. It is a war memorial, created to commemorate the lives of over 90,000 Indian soldiers who died in World War I and the Anglo-Afghan War. The inscription on the gate reads as follows:

> *'To the dead of the Indian Armies who fell and are honoured in France and Flanders Mesopotamia and Persia East Africa Gallipoli and elsewhere in the near and far east and in sacred memory also of those whose names are here recorded and who fell in India or the north-west Frontier and during the third Afghan War.'*

 ## THE LIFE OF A LATRINE SWEEPER

Sukha's story might seem unbelievable to you. Should you wish to read an account of how people like Sukha lived and were treated in the last century, you could read a book called *Untouchable* by Mulk Raj Anand, one of the early Indian writers to write in English. Published in 1935, it depicts a day in the life a sweeper named Bakha.

STORIES OF

SYMBOLS

AND

LANGUAGE

THE BRAVEHEART
OF ASSAM

1

DO OR DIE

'At a time when I am about to launch the biggest fight in my life, there can be no hatred for the British in my heart,' the faint voice of the Mahatma came cracking through the stale air in the overcrowded room of a remote village in August 1942, as the transistor on the table in the centre sprung to life. Young Kanakalata placed her hands over her mouth as she pressed her friend Mukunda's hand. It felt like a dream.

The village provision store of Barangabari in Assam, which could ordinarily accommodate no more than the owner Devi Prasad and his assistant Lakha, was now filled with at least four dozen people, who had crowded around a magical thing called the 'radio'. Sitting atop sacks of grain and chillies, boxes bursting with pulses and other provisions, a curious crowd stared wide-eyed and open-mouthed at the device, scarcely able to believe that it brought them the voice and words of Mahatma Gandhi, who was speaking thousands of miles away in Bombay!

Seventeen-year-old Kanakalata was reminded of her grandmother's stories where the voices of the gods came down from the heavens. 'If you want real freedom, you will have to come together and join the movement,' the voice of Gandhi emerged out of a black box on that wet rainy evening. 'Together, we will compel the British to leave! I call upon each of you to join me in pressing for the end of British Rule in India. It is time the British Quit India!'

The transistor croaked and crackled. Devi Prasad, who sat crouched beside it, fiddled around with one of the knobs on its panel. The device made some more crackling and static noises.

'Can you believe we just heard Mahatma Gandhi speak?' whispered Mukunda, turning to Kanakalata in delight.

Kanakalata shook her head in disbelief. It was unreal. Situated as they were, in a remote little village in Assam, news from the big cities usually got to them days after the events had occurred! And yet Kanakalata had followed them diligently, listening to every word her uncles discussed, her ears pricking up at words like Congress or Gandhi. The Congress Radio, which had just begun to provide regular updates on the Freedom Movement to Indians, had recently started its secret broadcast and was changing the pace at which young girls like Kanakalata could receive and respond to Gandhi's call for freedom.

'I say to the British . . .' Gandhi's voice streamed through again after a few moments, as the crowd moved closer so they could listen above the sound of the incessant rain. 'If you want help from us as friends, it's yours. But we are not servants. We do not want to be involved in your war. No Indian should help with the British war,' said Gandhi, referring to the war being fought by Britain in Europe. Kanakalata understood what Gandhi meant. Being a girl, she had been compelled to drop out of school early to help with household chores. But she knew that Europe was embroiled in a bitter war and that Indians were being asked to join in to fight for the British against the Germans.

'Absolutely right!' her maternal uncle exclaimed, clapping his hands together, 'Why should we die for Britain? Why must we die to fight for *their* freedom? For *their* war against the Germans? *Thoo!*' he spat on the floor in contempt. 'A lion hunting a deer wants help from the prey to fend off an attack from a hunter!' her uncle snorted.

'What more should you do?' Gandhi's voice came through once more. 'Every one of you should, from this moment onwards, consider yourself a free man or woman, and act as if you are free and are no longer under the heel of imperialism. The bond of the slave is snapped the moment he considers himself to be a free being!'

Kanakalata sat up, her back straight, head high and chin up. Looking over the shoulders of the people huddled in front of her, she looked straight at the transistor and felt the Mahatma was talking directly to her. No . . . she was no slave. And no one could force her into a life of slavery. Gandhi's message had found its mark.

'Here is a mantra that I give you,' the voice from the radio went on. 'You may imprint it in your heart and let every breath give expression to it. The mantra is "Do or Die". We shall either free India or *die* in the attempt. We shall not live to see the perpetuation of our slavery. Let every man and woman live every moment for achieving freedom. Take a pledge that you will no longer rest, till freedom is achieved and be prepared to lay down your lives to achieve it.'

Later that eventful night, as the rain kept pouring, Kanakalata Barua stood by the raging waters of the Brahmaputra and closed her tear-filled eyes. Standing in the cold rain, right arm crossed over her chest, the young seventeen-year-old took a silent vow.

'I will not rest until India is free and I am prepared to lay down my life for it!'

2

LIVING ON THE EDGE

'Never!' exclaimed Kanakalata's old grandfather, shaking his head in disbelief. The girl had lost both her parents—her mother when she was all but five and her father before she had turned thirteen. The responsibility to raise the child was on his aging shoulders. 'No,' he said firmly.

'But Dada . . .' Kanakalata pleaded, watching the flowing waters of the Luit River behind her home, 'thousands are joining Gandhiji's call to make the British leave India. I too want to be a part of this.'

'But you are a *girl*, Kanaka! This sort of work is not for you.'

'How does that make any difference?' Kanakalata argued back. 'Look at Pushpalata Das. She's a woman too. She has spent the last two years in jail fighting for our freedom!'

The old man shook his head. He was not prepared to argue about this. The girl could not go and that was the end of that.

'Has Kasturba not accompanied Gandhiji to jail, joining him in his struggle at every step?' Kanakalata went on. 'And Sarojini Naidu . . . and–'

'I don't know about all these people!' her grandfather said sternly, turning around to head back into the house. '*You* are not going!'

'Have you forgotten the sacrifice of Jaymati Kunwari?' Kanakalata asked, tailing him like a shadow. 'Has grandmother not been singing songs about her bravery to us since we were children? Jaymati was a woman too. But didn't she fight for her kingdom?'

'Look Kanaka,' said her grandfather, disturbed by his granddaughter's determination. 'You are seventeen now. It's time that I get you married. In fact, the question of your marriage has been on my mind for some time.'

'Please do not talk of marriage! How can I think of myself when my nation is in trouble, Dada?'

'This is not child's play!' her grandfather said calmly, putting his hand on the young girl's shoulders. 'The nation's problems cannot be solved by you!'

'Then who?' Kanakalata shot back. 'If each of us thinks so, how can anything change? Gandhiji has said—'

'Gandhiji may have said whatever he said!' the old man dismissed her remark with a wave of his hands. 'He talks of non-violence. But that is not what the British follow. The English do not care about Indian lives. You are too young to understand. Do you not know how many people—even well-known leaders like Lala Lajpat Rai—were brutally beaten by the police for participating in silent protests? They were harming nobody!'

'I am aware of the risk, Dada!' said Kanakalata, stopping to look him straight in the eye.

'Innocents have been beaten mercilessly . . . they've lost their lives,' the old man continued, shaking his head. 'And you are so young . . . you know nothing of the world.'

'I know,' Kanakalata nodded softly. 'Gandhiji's call is very clear. Do or Die. And . . . I . . . I am prepared to die!'

Kanakalata's grandfather stood frozen for a few moments, staring into the determined eyes of a girl he no longer recognized. Kanaka was far from the little girl who had wept herself to sleep after the death of her father or the little girl whom he carried on his shoulders for long walks along the river so she may get over the shock of her mother's death. Standing before him was a new girl . . . a woman: fierce and independent, someone who knew exactly what she wanted.

'I cannot give you permission, Birbala,' said the old man, using the name with which he often called his granddaughter affectionately. 'I cannot push you into your own funeral pyre!' he said, turning back with drooping shoulders.

Kanakalata clicked her teeth in disappointment and marched off. Finding her way to the little mound by the riverside, she sat down at her favourite spot. Where she always found peace when her mind was in turmoil. The waters of the Brahmaputra calmed her.

Suddenly, a flash of blue gliding above the water caught her eye. Kanaka smiled. Diving and rolling. Dipping and curving. No matter how often she saw the roller bird, it never failed to delight her. Worries about freedom were lost for a few moments in the realm of another world.

The roller bird finished its dip and flew straight in her direction. Kanaka sat still, for she knew any movement would cause the bird to fly away. Her eyes transfixed upon the spectacular speck of blue, she noticed the bird going straight up towards a branch of a tree beside her, where two little fledglings waited with their mouths open. Kanaka watched in delight as the baby birds slurped up the water from their mother's mouth.

Soon one of the young fledglings spread its wings, signalling its readiness to fly. Hopping towards the edge of the nest, it waited as its mother looked on. And then it made the dive! No doubt, it was hoping to slice through the air and roll just like its mother! But no sooner had the chick taken flight, that it fell to the ground with a thud. But the mother didn't seem alarmed. The other baby looked on with curiosity.

Oh you poor little thing, Kanaka thought to herself.

The little roller bird, no bigger than Kanaka's little palms, steadied itself on its two feet again and hopped a few steps to gain momentum. And once again, it spread its wings and lifted its body off the ground.

Kanaka's eyes lit up with a smile. Silently she edged the little bird on.

Thud! The little one fell back down again almost as soon as it had lifted off.

But Kanaka didn't fail to notice: the bird did not despair. Nor did the mother, watching patiently from the nest, do anything to encourage or discourage the youngling. Watching only over the safety of her young, the mother just let the little one be.

The little roller carried on and on. Trying again and again.

'Freedom! It is so dear to every creature!' said Kanaka to herself, admiring the resolve and determination of the little bird.

'One day soon,' she whispered to the little fledgling on the ground. 'One day soon, you shall be free! And so shall I!'

3

BRAVE NEW WORLD

'How does this radio work?' Kanakalata asked her uncle, as they walked towards Devi Prasad's store to listen to the secret transmission of the evening. 'It's such an amazing device!'

Kanakalata's uncle looked at his niece admiringly in the light of the torch in his hands. The young girl was up at the crack of dawn, collecting wood to start the kitchen fire, cleaning the house, helping her step-mother and aunts with the cooking, fetching water, attending to her younger siblings . . . And yet, she had the energy to enquire into matters beyond her mundane world, begging him each time to take her for the evening meetings at the grocery store where people discussed the freedom struggle.

'Well, it works on airwaves!' he replied, smiling at his curious niece. 'And a daredevil group of people in Bombay has managed to get a secret radio station going, through which they keep us informed about the news. The police are trying their best to locate them and so these people must constantly shift location to avoid getting caught!'

Kanakalata was baffled. Everything exciting and interesting seemed to be happening so far away. In the big cities. In Bombay.

Or in Calcutta. She wondered if she could do anything in her little village that counted for anything!

'We in Barangabari, Tezpur and other areas of Assam are planning to join the movement in a big way,' her uncle said, as they filled into Devi Prasad's little store, seating themselves beside the radio.

Slowly the others poured in. In the dim light of the lantern, Kanakalata scanned their eager faces. All of them young and raring to play their part, putting forth their suggestions on what can be done in Barangabari to take the struggle forward. Kanaka looked on with envy.

'Namaskar! This is the Congress Radio calling on 42.34 meters from somewhere in India . . .' a young female voice announced from the radio set. Kanakalata's eyes lit up. The voice sounded like that of a young girl, much like her! Kanakalata imagined the girl huddling in a secret location somewhere in the country, sending out the radio message to millions of listeners across India! Oh, why couldn't she do something thrilling like that?

'Earlier yesterday, it was announced that the All India Congress had adopted the Quit India Resolution and further, that a flag salutation ceremony would be held on the morning of 9 August at the Gowalia Tank Maidan,' the young lady's voice began defiantly. 'You also heard the call and announcement by Mahatma Gandhi about launching the movement.'

'But now, we bring you news about Gandhiji's arrest!' the tone turned melancholic. 'Gandhiji has been arrested in Bombay along with top ranking leaders of the Congress!'

A strange hush fell over the listeners. The light of the single lantern in Devi Prasad's store saw a blanket of gloom pulled over curious hopeful eyes. 'Gandhiji, Sardar Patel, Jawaharlal Nehru,

Maulana Azad, Rajendra Prasad, Acharya Kriplani and almost the entire top leadership of the Congress has been arrested and put behind bars by the British government that considers the Quit India Resolution to be a revolution against its government.'

A collective gasp was heard. Devi Prasad sat frozen in disbelief. Kanakalata's uncle slumped back holding his head. Mukunda turned to Kanaka in shock.

Nobody said a word.

'Harold Edwin Butler, the Commissioner of Police in Mumbai, personally went to arrest Gandhiji at 5 a.m. this morning,' the girl on the radio went on. 'Gandhiji was arrested from Birla house in Bombay early this morning and taken to Victoria Terminus accompanied by two police officers, to board a special train along with several others of the Bombay Congress and taken to an undisclosed location. We still have no information about Bapu's location.'

Kanaka's eyes went blurry. She had never seen Gandhiji but had seen pictures from the few Congress bulletins and newspapers that had managed to find their way into her remote village.

'As we report this unfortunate event, it also gives us great pride to report how young Indians have taken to the streets to keep alive the flame of the movement launched by Gandhiji,' the newsreader continued with a new resolve. 'Even as the leaders of the Congress were whisked away early this morning, Aruna Asaf Ali, a young firebrand leader, unfurled the national flag at the Gowalia Tank Maidan in Bombay. As soon as the police swooped down on the crowd, declaring the meeting illegal and giving thousands of people assembled there no more than two minutes to disperse, the young lady scrambled up to the dais, made an announcement to the people about Gandhi's arrest and hoisted the national flag. No sooner had the flag been unfurled that the police lobbed tear-gas shells into the crowd.'

Goosebumps covered Kanakalata's body. *Clearly, her dada was wrong! Women and girls everywhere were taking part in the freedom struggle*, she thought to herself. There was the brave young lady who was speaking on the radio despite the police trying to hunt her down. There was the other woman, who had hoisted the flag even when her tallest leaders had been whisked off to jail! Kanakalata was full of awe for the brave young woman who had torn through the ring of policemen and marched to the dais to hoist the flag.

'As news of Gandhi's arrest spread, the city of Bombay has plunged into *hartals*, processions and demonstrations . . . Signs of popular unrest are everywhere. The government has taken recourse to mass arresting and firing, leading to further chaos and disorder. Unrest is fast spreading into the interiors of Bombay Presidency and other provinces. News, of attempts across the country to raid police stations, post offices and railway stations, has been coming in.'

A veil of tension gripped the listeners as they huddled about in shock in the dingy provision store, the rain beginning to pelt in sheets above them.

'As we protest the arrest of Gandhi, it would be fit to remember his words,' the young girl continued, her voice firm and resolute. 'Only yesterday, Gandhi urged every Indian who desired freedom, including all students above sixteen years of age, to come out of their schools and colleges and not return to them till after independence. The nation needs you NOW!'

TAKING THE PLUNGE

'From this day on, we shall be known as the Mrityu Bahini!' the announcement sounded like a sudden clap of thunder on a dark dreary night.

Kanakalata's breath froze.

Mrityu Bahini—Death Squad.

The words hit her with a jolt.

Do or Die. Do or Die. Do or Die.

Those words were doing the rounds ever since Gandhiji first gave the call a week ago. But it had seemed distant then. Like a cloudburst over a land far away. She had felt envious then, looking on at the burst of showers, wondering if the rain would ever quench her thirst. But now it felt more intimate. The thunderstorm was approaching.

Pushpalata Das, the firebrand Congress leader from Assam, who had bravely courted arrest, was speaking at the secret meeting at the *kirtan ghar*. Dozens of people were huddled around a rickety table at the centre of the hall. There was palpable excitement in the air. People were raring to go. To join their countrymen in the march to freedom. To do something worthwhile with their youth and their energy.

'Do not take Birbala to these meetings!' Kanakalata's grandfather had scolded her uncle, earlier that day. 'She is young and impressionable! And she has a whole life ahead of her. Do not get her involved with things that are not within her domain,' he had warned.

But Kanakalata had other plans. Completing all the household chores so her absence would not be noticed, she and Mukunda had hurried to the kirtan ghar when it had become known that the famous leaders Pushpalata Das and Jyoti Prasad Agarwala were coming to the village to address a secret meeting.

Kanakalata stood on her toes to get a glimpse of the action. 'We must run the movement non-violently and then proceed to the thanas of Tezpur to hoist the Congress flag, sloganeering Quit India,' Das continued her speech. As Kanaka watched Das, dressed in a white cotton handspun saree, holding her fort amidst men, she was filled with awe.

'India has tolerated injustice for a long time but it need not do so forever. We must fight. It will not be easy. We will have to suffer. We may be arrested or even killed. We must be prepared.'

Yes. Kanaka had heard that before. But suddenly the meaning of it came roaring home.

'We will hoist the Congress flag in government buildings and police stations,' Agarwala spoke up now. 'Let this be the first province to lower the British flag and fly a national flag in its place! Let it become a symbol of freedom for the people of the world. Gandhiji has said that hoisting the flag is not just a ceremony. It is an embodiment of all that we cherish and honour. Once the flag is hoisted, it should not be lowered, no matter what—even if we have to die for it! And we will not be afraid to offer our blood on the altar of liberation for our motherland!'

'Victory to the swadeshis! Victory to the flag! Victory through non-violence!' the crowds shouted.

Kanakalata revelled in the surge of excitement that rose all round her. 'Victory to the flag! Victory to the flag!' she joined the chorus.

The battle lines were drawn. The moment of reckoning was upon her. It was down to the mantra.

Do or Die!

5

D-DAY

As the first light of dawn filled the sky on 20 September 1942, Kanakalata rushed out to her special spot by the riverside. Folding her hands, she bowed before the mighty Brahmaputra. *Give me strength,* she prayed.

With closed eyes, she listened for a few moments to the reassuring sound of the water gushing by. Somewhere within her, doubts arose. She wondered if she'd ever hear that sound again. Brushing away the thought, Kanakalata took a deep breath and a wave of inspiration filled her lungs. *No fear.*

Balancing for a moment atop the little mound before turning back home, Kanaka peeped into the nest of the roller. Both fledglings had grown now. They were as large as their mother and looked like they were ready to take on the world.

'Soon,' she said, turning back to the birds as she walked home, 'Soon, we shall all be free!'

Finishing all her household chores as usual, Kanakalata slipped out of the house, not wanting to say anything that might rouse her grandfather's suspicion. She looked back at her home— at her family, her grandparents, her step mother and her siblings, who loved her dearly. The doubt in her mind reared its head once more. She shrugged and walked on.

'Are you going to the town square for the protest?' a young girl, no older than her, asked on the way. Kanakalata just nodded.

'I'm Indulekha,' she said, introducing herself. 'We are from Kalabari. My friends and I have come from school to join the march.'

'Welcome,' smiled Kanaka. 'You can come along with me.'

'And that group there—300 of them have walked for more than a day to join this march,' Indulekha added, pointing to a large troop of girls walking behind them.

Kanakalata felt reassured to see so many young girls like her. They had come from far but they had one thing in common: the dream of freedom.

'Remember . . . our march is to be non-violent,' Jyoti Prasad Agarwala was addressing the crowd when Kanaka reached the square. 'We will raise the national flag in courts and police stations but we will not forget Gandhi's words. This is going to be peaceful. Even if we are hit, we will not hit back!'

Taking a deep breath, Kanakalata took her position at the head of the procession that was to march towards the Gohpur Police Station. Mukunda filed in behind her. The friends hugged one another. Millions were rising to Gandhi's call. Thousands had come from great distances to join the march. They were all young like her. Young and spirited. And she had been given pride of place in leading these youngsters and hoisting the flag. It was the moment she had always waited for.

'Vande Maataram! Vande Maataram! Vande Maataram!' a chorus of voices began chanting as Kanakalata and her large troupe of little women dressed in white sarees saluted the flag and began marching silently to various destinations.

Picking up the flag pole, Kanakalata looked up and smiled. The flag gently waving in the breeze soothed her senses like the caressing hands of her grandmother. She walked on fearlessly, leading the way, with hundreds behind her, the song of freedom in their hearts and the spring of youth in their steps.

Just as they turned the bend before the police station, the broad frame of Officer Som blocked her path. 'I am warning you all,' his booming voice thundered through the little funnel-shaped microphone he held in front of his mouth, to make himself audible. 'Do not proceed or else I will be forced to take action.'

Kanakalata turned to face him, noticing his stern features and his team of a dozen fierce-looking policemen men standing behind him. They were all holding wooden sticks in their hands, ready to rain down blows on the young girls. She could hear her heart beating loudly within her ribs.

Do or Die. Do or Die. The call of Gandhiji echoed in her ears.

'Vande Maataram!' she cried out with gusto. 'Angrezon Bharat Chodo!'

Two policemen rushed forward with sticks. She closed her eyes but did not cower.

'Why are you at somebody's feet? Why is your head bowed?' the words of their leader Agarwala came rushing into her mind.

'Vande Maataram!' Mukunda and the other girls behind her raised a chorus.

The vision of Aruna Asaf Ali hoisting the flag amidst lathi-charging and gun-wielding policemen appeared before Kanakalata. Mukunda's presence and voice behind her gave her added strength. She marched on, her breath quickening, disregarding the warnings, her gaze intent on the flag she held high in her hands.

'Do not forget the sacrifice of Jaymati!' Kanakalata urged the girls standing behind her. 'Don't be scared! We are not slaves! This is *our* home. We will live as free people in a free nation!'

Climbing atop the platform within the compound of the police thana, Kanakalata raised the bamboo pole.

'Vande Maatram! Vande Maataram!' the slogan rented the air.

'Stop! I order you to stop!' yelled Officer Som, his eyes flashing red. His junior officers stood in line, ready to spring into action at their superior's command. 'Back off, or else you will regret your actions.'

Kanakalata stood still for a moment. Just then, a flash of blue in the distance caught her attention. Two roller birds were dipping and rolling in the southern skies. *Freedom at last*, she smiled to herself, watching the antics of the two fledglings who were experiencing the joy of flight. Officer Som's voice faded into the background. '*We* are free!' she whispered to the birds in the distance.

Kanakalata mounted the platform and raised her right hand high. Her lips parted in a subtle smile, tears welled up in her eyes, her throat choked with emotion.

As she stepped up to begin hoisting the flag atop the district police station, she felt a moment of stillness amidst the din of people shouting and raising slogans all around her. The voice of the police officer was muted out. The chorus of the slogans died down. For a second, she experienced bliss.

For a second and no more.

Suddenly there was a boom, like the clap of thunder.

Bang!

Something sharp pierced Kanakalata's chest. An excruciating pain filled her lungs. Kanaka looked down at her blood-soaked saree.

'Ahhh . . .' she let out a gasp, before stumbling and collapsing into the arms of Mukunda, who stood behind her.

'Hold on to the flag,' Kanakalata whispered to her friend, her face contorted in agony. 'The flag must not fall!'

Young Mukunda doddered under the weight of her friend. But she took hold of the bamboo staff that held the flag aloft.

'Vande Mataram!' the girls shouted in unison, as Mukunda stepped forward with the flag, unmoved, undeterred and fearless.

Bang!

A bullet pierced Mukunda's back. The young girl collapsed over her friend in a heap, their white sarees turning red.

Young Indulekha, standing behind Mukunda, went ahead, undaunted by the dying cries of her two companions, unmindful of the fate that no doubt awaited her if she dared to take the next step. Holding the flag pole, she stepped forward.

Bang! Bang! Bang! Bang!

Soon, there were piles of dead bodies, the earth beneath stained with the colour of blood.

Each of the young girls went down with the flag held high. Passing it on to the next in line before a bullet robbed them of their lives. Not one of them fought back. Not one of them turned on the police. Not one of the let out an abusive word or cry or curse. Like trained soldiers, they followed their oath and sacrificed themselves for what they held so dear.

Freedom.

Kanakalata's frail fingers reached out to Mukunda, who lay on the ground beside her, writhing in pain. The two friends who had held hands through their many joys, held hands one last time, as life slowly dimmed out of their veins.

The acrid smell of gunfire and smoke filled the air. Kanakalata could hear screams, gunshots and shuffling feet all around her. A tear rolled down her eyes as she saw in the skies the faces of her parents, calling out to her. And then she smiled, seeing that one vision she had often seen in her dreams.

The tricolour flying high.

Only this time, it was not a dream.

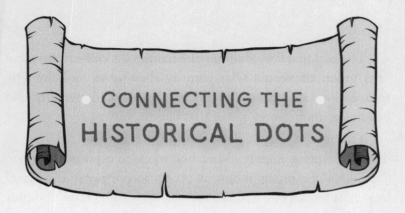

CONNECTING THE
HISTORICAL DOTS

 THE MEANING OF SYMBOLS

A young seventeen-year-old girl gives up her life to hoist a flag!

You might wonder *why* and *how*, a flag—which is a symbol—could evoke such intense feeling and passion.

To understand the place that symbols have in our lives, let's examine some other examples: =, @, &, % and so on.

Common symbols you encounter in your daily life. They have meaning and purpose. But clearly, they do not evoke any emotion because they are meant for standard everyday usage.

How about a logo like that of Coca-Cola? A mark like the cross in a church? The national flag?

The logo of Coca-Cola becomes symbolic of the drink and the company. It creates a certain impression in your mind.

The cross becomes a representative of Jesus Christ and his sacrifice. It evokes a certain feeling in a devout Christian.

The national flag of a country becomes the collective symbol of a group of people who identify themselves as belonging to a nation. It evokes ideas of brotherhood, nationality and belonging amongst people of that nation.

The reason these symbols evolved relates to the human desire to express oneself. When one wants to express a concrete idea like a star or the moon, it is easy to portray it as a visual image. But when one wishes to convey something more complex like pain or hunger, a symbol can be useful.

And so, a heart becomes the symbol of love. A red octagon, the symbol for stop. A flag becomes the symbol of freedom. In other words, a symbol is one thing that stands for another.

In fact, all communication takes place only through the use of symbols—including the words you are currently reading. These words are symbols that find their meaning only in the reader's brain. To a person who does not read the english language, these are but marks on one page that carry no meaning at all. Just like words in a language you do not read will bear no meaning for you.

So, when you read Kanakalata's story, you may wonder why so many young people gave up their lives to hoist a flag. But that is not for the flag in itself. It is because the flag was a symbol of something else. And we may do well to remember their sacrifice to this greater cause – which is the bedrock of our freedom.

Even today, symbols like national flags, religious icons and political party symbols can evoke intense emotions in people for they are representations of a deeper idea or ideology which people hold dear or feel strongly about.

What kinds of symbols do you find in your life? What meaning is attached to these symbols? How did they acquire that meaning? How do you feel about those symbols? Can you think of expressing yourself without the use of symbols?

UNBOX THE PAST: DISCOVER HISTORY HIDDEN IN THE STORY.

 QUIT INDIA MOVEMENT

World War II broke out in September 1939 when Hitler invaded Poland. Britain was forced to join the war and pulled in its forces from India, without consulting the Congress or elected members of the Central Legislature.

Three decades earlier, India had helped Britain during World War I (1914–18), after which Britain failed to keep the promises it had made to India to win her support.

Feeling cheated, Indian leaders were sceptical about supporting Britain in World War II. They offered to cooperate, provided Britain promised complete independence after the war.

Desperate for India's cooperation in the war effort, a mission was sent to India under Sir Strafford Cripps, known as the Cripps Mission. However, the British government refused to accept the Congress' demand for an immediate transfer of power to Indians, resulting in the failure of the Cripps Mission.

In view of these developments, the Congress decided to take active steps to push the British into leaving India. As a result, on 8 August 1942, the All India Congress Committee met in Bombay and passed the famous Quit India Resolution under which Mahatma Gandhi gave the famous mantra, 'Do or Die'.

However, even before the Congress would start the movement, early on 9 August 1942, Gandhi and other Congress leaders were arrested.

News of the arrest spread fast. People spontaneously came out to protest. There were strikes and demonstrations. Symbols of British authority such as police stations, post offices and railway stations, telegraph and telephone wires, railway lines and government buildings became the subject of public anger. People marched to these buildings and hoisted the Indian flag.

The British administration repressed and crushed the movement. Demonstrating crowds were machine-gunned and bombed from the air. The military took over many towns and cities. Mass floggings were held in villages and the rebellious were made to pay huge sums as fines. It is said that over 10,000 people died in police and military firings.

 ## THE ROLE OF THE RADIO

In today's age, where information is so easily and openly available, it is perhaps difficult to imagine how the leaders of our freedom movement managed to reach out to people across such a vast geographic space in a time when such technology was not available.

One of the highlights of the Quit India movement was the Congress Radio that gave regular updates of national and international news to people. Vithaldas Khakkhar, Usha Mehta, Vithaldas Jhaveri, Nanak Motwane and Chandrakant Jhaveri were some of the people involved with the effort. They were helped by leaders such as Ram Manohar Lohia.

The team had to keep changing their place of transmission in order to avoid getting caught by the police.

The radio station was on air from the mid-August until 12 November 1942, when the police raided the place of transmission, arresting the members and framing charges against them. Many of those involved were sentenced to rigorous imprisonment.

 ## SHOT DEAD FOR HOISTING THE FLAG

On 8 August 1942, Mahatma Gandhi gave the historic call, demanding that the British quit India, urging people 'to do or die' for the freedom of the country.

Early the next morning, the top leadership of the Congress was arrested. Aruna Asaf Ali, a young girl, came forward to hoist the tricolour at the Gowalia Tank Maidan in Bombay, even as the police lathi charged and fired bullets into the crowd.

Hoisting of the flag was made a crime by the British, liable to two years imprisonment. However, people openly defied the orders and several youngsters, including seventeen-year-old Kanakalata Barua and her friend Mukunda were killed by the police for hoisting the flag in Tezpur, Assam.

Many other youngsters across the country faced the same fate as Kanakalata, shot dead for hoisting the flag. Thousands were beaten and arrested.

 ## WHAT'S IN A FLAG?

Have you noticed what all nations have in common?

A distinct national flag is one of the traits of a modern nation.

A flag is symbol of nationhood. A national anthem is another. These symbols evoke deep emotions and reactions like kinship and brotherhood, loyalty and sacrifice.

While the flag we recognize today as the Indian National Flag, came into existence only in July 1947, there were other flags that were in circulation prior to that. These flags acted as important rallying points during the struggle. It stood for something more than a piece of cloth: the idea of India.

 ## EVOLUTION OF THE INDIAN FLAG

The Indian National Flag evolved over a period of time during the anti-colonial struggle.

Between 1920 and 1947, several versions of the flag existed and detailed discussions took place over its design, size, colour components, symbolism and so on.

When India was to become independent, a committee was set up to suggest a flag for the free young nation. After discussions relating to various matters from the acceptability of the flag to various parties and communities to the diameter and size of the forms, the committee adopted the current flag that we have as the Indian National Flag. Mahatma Gandhi was not happy with the design of the flag as it did not contain the charkha.

 ## CODE FOR THE INDIAN FLAG

The Indian Flag is governed by strict rules and specifications, known as the Indian Standard.

The regulations lay down precise provisions such as the material of the flag, the count of yarn warp and weft, colour fastness to light, requirements of hemp cordage, lock stitches and various other details.

Apart from this, there is the Flag Code of India, which lays down rules for the display of the flag, do's and don'ts related to the hoisting and flying of the flag.

THE HARBINGER
OF ENGLISH

1

THE DARKNESS OF THE EAST

'He dares to come on board with nothing on him but a pointed yellow cap!' Macaulay exclaimed, holding back his sister Hannah. Looking over the railing of the ship which had dropped anchor outside Madras, the Englishman was horrified at the first sight of the half-naked Indian.

'The man is completely naked waist up!' Hannah giggled as they all stared in disbelief, unable to fathom how a man might so nonchalantly walk about shirtless in public.

'Tch! How shameless he must be to approach the ladies, without a care in the world about his state of undress!' sniggered another Englishman standing behind them.

'Oh, Lord! Help!' Macaulay laughed, holding his stomach, 'Only a small piece of rag to cover his modesty! I should think one will nearly die of laughter!'

The frail boatman did not understand a word of what the English sahibs and madams were saying. For his part, he thought *their* dress rather odd, and tried his best not to stare! They were not the first white people he had seen. There were already a few hundred of them in the city. But every time he did see them, he found their ways rather strange. He had often wondered why they dressed so peculiarly—the women in thick rustling gowns and the men in silk stockings and tight shoes. *How do they wear so many layers of clothing and cover themselves from head to toe in this sweltering heat? No air can pass through their clothes. No wonder they are constantly falling sick!* he thought to himself, as he rowed, guiding his boat to the shore.

Grudgingly taking the boatman's hand and immediately wiping it off on his jacket, the stout Macaulay hauled himself ashore, before extending his hand to his sister Hannah and the ladies who cringed in embarrassment to touch the half-naked man. Stepping on the beach, Macaulay turned to look at the waterfront of the land that was to be his new home.

Meh! Little impressed him—the heat was oppressive, the architecture strange and the air smelt like that of a hothouse! The trees and flowers were unlike anything he had seen in England.

Now, this is going to be something . . . An utterly depressing posting, this one . . . he thought, sighing as he walked up to the end of the beach, towards the carriage waiting to take him to the governor's guest-house. But Macaulay needed this job. He needed the money. He needed the opportunity. The chance to prove his mettle. He needed the chance to shine.

'What in heaven's name!' shrieked Hannah, holding her brother's arm and stepping back in dismay. A horde of barely-clad men stood at the edge of the beach. Jugglers with cups and balls, conjurers with swords and ropes, snake-charmers with baskets filled with hissing cobras. A motley audience stood around them, laughing and clapping.

A young girl was walking on a rope mounted at a great height, balancing a long pole of bamboo in her hands. A monkey performed to the beat of a tambourine under a large tree. An acrobat jumped and juggled five mangoes at once. A snake-charmer played a flute-like instrument to lure snakes out of his basket and dance to his tune.

The newly arrived Englishmen watched in fascination and horror. Hannah was amused and threw her head back and laughed. Macaulay smiled, pleased to see his sister forget her homesickness for the moment; the journey had been hard on her and not a day had gone by when she hadn't felt seasick. Yet, he couldn't approve of this kind of nonsense, which passed for entertainment. He had read about how witchcraft and sorcery were practised by the uncultured and uneducated and was deeply suspicious of this breed of tricksters.

How uncivil and crude, Macaulay thought to himself. He had spent the better part of his journey from England reading the Greek classics and the works of great Roman orators. *To have to land here after that!*

And then suddenly, as he settled into his carriage, he felt as if he had found a purpose. His role in the larger picture emerged with greater clarity before him. *India needs the British*, he said to himself. *Britain's civilizing influence would be a blessing to these unsophisticated people.* And he would be the torchbearer to take the light of the West to illuminate the darkness of the East.

2

COMMON CAUSE

'Good morning Mr Macaulay! It is a pleasure to have you here,' the governor-general of India, William Bentinck, welcomed the visitor as he emerged from the palanquin, borne by four muscular Indians up the rugged mountain slopes.

Macaulay put on his hat and stepped on the patio of the large mansion and took the governor-general's hand. 'I am greatly pleased to meet you,' he replied with a slight smile. Macaulay had heard much about Bentinck. He knew he was widely disliked. The governor-general routinely ignored the advice of the East India Company's bureaucrats and Macaulay was wary in his approach.

'How was your journey?' Bentinck enquired.

'The journey here from Madras was agreeable,' said Macaulay, nodding and glancing at his retinue of a dozen porters and officers who had carried him up to Ootacamund, the lovely hill retreat in the Nilgiri Hills where the governor-general was residing at the time. 'But . . .' he paused.

'Yes?' asked Bentinck, leading Macaulay into the massive house.

'To be on land after four months at sea is wonderful! But to be on *such* a land!' scoffed Macaulay with a shrug of his shoulders. Neither the spectacular view of the valley nor the sweet song of the whistling thrush caught his attention.

'What do you mean?'

'Oh! The dark faces and white turbans. The trees, so unlike our own. The very smell of the place. The absurd architecture. Stranger than the vegetation!'

'Come, come!' Bentinck smiled, leading Macaulay into the living room. 'It's not so bad!'

'The music is deplorable!' Macaulay continued. 'Vocal or instrumental, which one is worse I cannot decide! It all sounds awful—much like the noise of a kettle beaten with a poker!'

Bentinck laughed. 'Just as the weather in these hills has shown you a different side to this country, perhaps, you might change your mind about the rest too! Have you tasted these local fruits?' he asked, pointing to a tray of neatly arranged fruits in the living room. 'I assure you your heart will delight in them!'

Macaulay winced and turned up his face. 'The mango is the most displeasing thing I've ever eaten! And so is that rotten thing they call the banana! Nothing at all like the strawberries and grapes we get back at home!' he brooded. 'And don't even get me started on the oppressive heat,' he added, following Bentinck into the veranda.

'That's the reason I asked that you come up here,' said Bentinck, pointing to the mist-filled valley below. 'This place is lovely. The weather is cool—much like it is back in England.'

Macaulay nodded. He had to grudgingly admit that the scenery was magnificent beyond description and the temperature much like that of England. 'On the weather, I must admit . . . I never knew what thunder and lightning were till I came to India! But . . . the people,' he continued, not quite done with his tirade. 'The people of India are like children! Nothing civil or noble or refined about any of them! I was appalled to find them worshiping this bizarre figure they call Ganesha! A fat man with a paunch— with an elephant's head no less! And a trunk and a dozen hands and a mouse! Would you believe it? It shows how primitive they are!'

Bentinck continued to listen, sizing up Macaulay, for putting in place his own plans for India—for his ambitious program to introduce liberal reforms in India's traditions and customs. He had already worked with Indian leaders like Raja Ram Mohan Roy to abolish Sati, the practice where a widow burnt herself on her husband's pyre upon his death. Yes, he could empathize with Macaulay. He too had been dismayed and horrified when he had first arrived. He tried to read the young man. *Something tells me he's the right man for the job.*

'The palaces of their kings look like toy shops!' Macaulay went on, as he seated himself on a large sofa in the veranda. 'The roof, the walls, the pillars, the railings—all so gaudy. Their architecture is so vulgar and lacking in taste!'

'All right! All right, my man!' Bentinck smiled, taking a seat. 'Let's get to work, shall we? That might put your mind beyond these matters of discomfort better than anything else.'

Macaulay couldn't agree more. He was raring to go.

'I wish to discuss an urgent matter with you,' began Bentinck, 'I realize you have only just arrived. But I'd rather have this out of the way. As you are no doubt aware, the East India Company allocates government funds for the support of teaching and colleges. It has been a policy since 1813.'

Macaulay nodded slightly. He had spent the last few years keenly following the goings-on in India. He knew everything there was to know.

'However, the question of government-supported education has come under the scanner lately,' Bentinck continued. 'The voices of one section—the Anglicists—are getting louder. They insist that the funds of the East India Company are better used in supporting what they call "useful learning" over native learning. And that English be introduced in Indian schools and colleges.'

'But of course! What's the issue with *that*?'

'The Orientalists! They have an issue with that!' quipped Bentinck, carefully noting Macaulay's every reaction. 'They say that government funds ought to be set aside for paying stipends to students at colleges where Arabic and Sanskrit are being taught! They support traditional teaching. And demand that sciences and arts be taught in native Indian languages and not in English.'

Macaulay shifted about on the sofa. He had heard of the Orientalists. Some of them were fine scholarly Englishmen like Sir William Jones. They claimed that they had discovered, in Indian literature, sublime works like the Greek classics. Macaulay scoffed.

'On my part,' Bentinck said, gazing out into the distance, 'I am convinced that the acquisition by Indians of the English language is the key to all improvement. What are your views on the matter?'

Macaulay couldn't hide his smile. Here was a man whose thoughts appeared to reflect his own.

'I have been in India only a few weeks,' Macaulay began. 'But the time I have spent here is enough for me to have understood that it is essential that the government takes charge of educating the people of this land. I had the opportunity to meet rulers and nawabs during my short stay. I could scarcely suppress my laughter at the nonsense they speak! It is imperative that our government educate Indians the way we educate English children back home. We *need* to civilize these people!'

'I am glad to see you agree with my views Mr Macaulay,' noted the governor-general, stroking his chin. 'To tell you the truth, this is a policy that has economic effects. I am in favour of hiring more Indians and less Englishmen in the administration. It costs the Company far less to have things that way. And if I am to push this through, I need English to be taught to Indians. You understand what I'm saying?'

'Absolutely!' agreed Macaulay. 'To be honest, I am appalled at the argument of the Orientalists to introduce education in the manner of the natives. We must promote western education amongst the population. We must communicate Europe's learning and bring the benefits of its civilization to Indians.'

'Certainly!' nodded Bentinck, pleased to note Macaulay's strong views on the matter. 'That would also help promote loyalty amongst Indians to British rule. Anyway, matters have come to a head now. The Anglicists and the Orientalists will be presenting their arguments before the Committee of Public Instruction. At the moment, there is a deadlock in the Committee. It is divided five against five.'

Macaulay was taken aback. He hadn't expected it to be this close. The matter appeared like a non-issue to him. *Who in their right minds would object to Western education? And the introduction of English?* It was beyond him.

'Of the Committee members—Messer's Bird, Bushby, Colvin, Saunders and Trevelyan are not a problem. As I understand, Mr Charles Trevelyan—is your sister's fiancé? Yes?'

Macaulay nodded. Charles would need no convincing. He already belonged to the pro-English language camp.

'Now the old members of the Committee are Messer's Shakespear, MacNaughten, Sutherland, J Princep and H.T. Princep—they all favour the Orientalist program,' Bentinck paused to observe Macaulay's expression. He was hoping, if he played his cards well, he could still have his way.

Bentinck had already taken due precaution by sending off H.T. Princep, one of the most vocal supporters of the Orientalists, to a commission in Tasmania at the right time. The numbers should now favour him. But he didn't want to take a chance.

'And what is it that I am supposed to do? Break this deadlock?' Macaulay cut into Bentinck's thoughts.

'My dear Macaulay, I wish for you to be appointed . . . as the President of the Committee.'

'What?' Macaulay raised his eyebrows. He hadn't anticipated this. Bentinck watched Macaulay's face carefully. He was hoping that appointing Macaulay as the President of the Committee would turn things in his favour with the crucial casting vote.

'You can take some time to think it over,' suggested Bentinck.

There was a short pause as the koel filled the air with her sorrowful notes. Despite the cool mountain air, Macaulay felt warm and loosened his necktie. His heart began to beat faster. The opportunity he had waited for—to leave his mark in history . . . *here it was!*

'No, no! No time is to be wasted in *thinking*,' Macaulay responded quickly. 'I am honoured by the confidence you place in me, Governor General. I shall leave for Calcutta immediately and start forthwith. Whatever power I have shall be exerted towards this cause!'

Bentinck smiled and sat back, relaxed. Perhaps the deadlock would end in a way he wanted after all.

For the first time since his arrival, Macaulay felt he had no reason to curse and complain. He even noticed the whistling thrush and found a reason to smile.

3

MACAULAY'S CHILDREN

'I do not understand how *you* can support teaching only Hindu and Muslim classics at University!' fumed Macaulay, glaring at the visitor sitting across his desk. 'Have you read them?'

'The question is Mr Macaulay,' replied Tytler, the champion of the Oriental cause, 'have *you* read them?'

John Tytler was not a part of the Committee of Public Instruction. And yet, Macaulay had agreed to meet the man. For the assistant surgeon had drawn his attention by his long letters and Macaulay thought it fit to give him a few minutes.

'In fact, if I may ask, do you have any knowledge of Sanskrit or Arabic at all to make such far-reaching statements?' Tytler asked boldly.

'Well, I must admit I know neither Sanskrit nor Arabic nor Persian,' Macaulay admitted rather proudly. 'But I am convinced, however, that there is little I stand to gain by learning these languages. It may nonetheless be said that I have a correct estimate of their value.'

'*You*, my dear sir, are not in a position to make such a statement if you don't know these languages.' Tytler said angrily.

'For Christ's sake!' Macaulay thumped the table with his palms before getting up in a flash. 'Their history abounds with kings 30 feet high and reigns 30,000 years long! And their geography—it is preposterous! It is made up of seas of treacle and butter! Does it matter in what grammar one talks nonsense?' Macaulay fumed as he paced up and down the room. 'Have you heard the ridiculous tales they spin? The world they say was surrounded by a sea of butter! They claim Mount Meru is the centre of the universe! Do you want such nonsense to be taught in schools? Is there *one* rational thought or idea in their literature? Any accurate knowledge or information that can compare with the noble works of Greece bequeathed to us?'

'They have great works of astronomy and mathematics here. If I can tell you about. . .' Tytler started.

'Look,' Macaulay cut him off, returning to his desk. 'English has access to all the vast knowledge of the earth. Sanskrit, Arabic and all the native languages of India are defective . . . they do not bear the knowledge carried by European languages for centuries. Native Indian learning only breeds ignorance and barbarism. Show me anything written in their languages that deserves being studied!'

'How can I show you if you don't know *how* to read them?'

'You mean to tell me if I could read these languages, I would find in them, classics like the plays of Sophocles and Thucydides and the works of Plato and Plutarch? Bah!'

'I request you to read the works of Kalidasa and Bhasa. In fact, none other than Sir William Jones, one of our most respected countrymen, has translated Kalidasa's work into English. I would recommend that you read–'

'And what will I find in there?' scoffed Macaulay. 'Some more nonsense about gods looking like elephants. Please, let's not waste time!'

Tytler turned away. *Macaulay's mind was closed!* He understood why Bentinck had chosen him to be President of the Committee. The letters and meetings were not going to help. He needed to try a different tack.

'Do you not agree that the point of an education is imparting useful knowledge to students?' Macaulay asked pointedly as he sat down, before Tytler could try an alternative approach.

'I do not contest that!' Tytler replied tersely.

'Then what is your case? Do you think teaching Sanskrit and Arabic and Persian is useful?'

'Look,' said Tytler, drawing closer to the table, 'We have no objection to the teaching of western science and philosophy. Only the medium of instruction that you insist upon. Surely, the sciences and all useful learning can be translated into Indian languages and taught to the people in their own mother tongue. Surely, you understand that children learn best in their own mother tongue.'

Macaulay shook his head. 'And how do you propose to carry out this enormous exercise? Where are the funds?'

'That is a small hurdle, Mr Macaulay. I'm sure it can be arranged . . .'

'That is not the only point of difficulty,' Macaulay pointed out. 'Dozens of languages, if not more, are spoken across India. Into which language will you translate our sciences?'

Tytler remained silent. It was a valid objection. There being no single Indian language, the works will need to be translated into dozens of languages for it to reach people everywhere. It was not going to be easy by any means.

'The knowledge that we wish to impart in India—mathematics and science, philosophy and art—it is all in the English language. English is the key that will open the window to all that vast knowledge. The languages of India simply do not have the adequate and precise words or terms to explain these ideas.' Macaulay went on.

'*That*, Mr Macaulay,' said Tytler forcefully, 'is an assumption you make. An incorrect one at that. Besides, you also underestimate the languages of India. India has a rich history of languages. Bengali alone is spoken by over 37 million people. It has good dictionaries and grammar and great written works of literature. As do Sanskrit and Persian. I assure you they have words that can carry the weight of any ideas taught in European schools.'

Macaulay waved off the idea and turning to look out of the window.

'I call upon you, sir, and upon your fraternity, to reconsider,' said Tytler, rising from his chair, knowing there was nothing left to discuss. 'Please do give my petition some thought. The future of an entire people lays in your hands. Not only will it cause great difficulty for the students in India. They will need to learn in a language that is not their mother tongue, but it would also result in the emergence of a new class of Indians that speak English, but not know their *own* languages.'

Macaulay stared out of the window in silence as Tytler made his way out. *A new class of Indians*—that is what he hoped to create. A class that could act as interpreters between the British and the rest of India. A class that was English in taste and values though Indian in flesh and blood.

He gazed into the distance, almost as if he were looking into the future. He could almost see them—a new class of Indians. 'They would take pride in reciting Shakespeare and Wordsworth!

They would compose letters and essays just like English children. They would speak and write in English with confidence,' Macaulay mumbled to himself proudly. 'So what if they forget their own languages? It is no great loss!'

Yes . . . he was certain that a new class of Indians would emerge. They would be his creation.

His children.

Macaulay's children.

4

SENSE OVER NONSENSE

'You are going to love this!' gushed Hannah, leading her brother by his elbow towards the vast public grounds behind their home.

'Oh, Hannah! I am tired,' pleaded Macaulay, 'Perhaps some other time.'

'You are always working or reading!' protested Hannah. 'Oh, please do come. For my sake!'

'My dear Hannah . . . you know I find no pleasure in these dancing bears and monkeys,' Macaulay tried to pull away.

'I promise you will enjoy this one,' said Hannah. 'This is better than anything you've ever seen . . . no dancing bears and monkeys this time!'

Macaulay couldn't wait to return to his study at the end of the day and continue reading the great speeches of Cicero that lay upon his desk. But his sisters, Hannah and Margaret, were the centre of his existence and he found it impossible to refuse them. He followed Hannah reluctantly.

A few dozen Englishmen and several locals were milling around a makeshift wooden platform at one end of the maidan, upon which sat a lanky brown man, clad only in a dhoti. The man on the stage was holding a vial in his hand from which he was pouring oil into his right palm, which was cupped. Bending forward, he drew out a sword that lay before him, about 20 inches in length, and rubbed the oil on its surface.

'Oh my!' exclaimed Hannah, raising her eyebrows. They took their seats and continued to watch. 'I wonder what he's going to do!'

The man on the stage appeared to be saying a silent prayer after which he threw his head back, holding the sword over his mouth, clasping it with both hands. He then carefully lowered the tip of the sword into his mouth, which he held wide open.

'No way!' Hannah squeezed her brother's hand in anticipation.

The man on stage pushed the sword down his throat. Further and further, more of it disappeared into his body.

'Oh dear Lord Jesus!' Hannah shrieked, holding her hands over her mouth. Her eyes were wide with fright.

When nothing but the hilt of the sword remained outside his mouth, the man let go of the handle and spread his arms wide apart. The rest of it had been swallowed. Despite his disdain for such performances, Macaulay found himself drawn in by the spectacle, leaning forward and craning his neck to get a better look.

'This is impossible!' the crowd gushed as an Englishman from amongst the spectators stepped upon the stage to take a closer look. He went near the performer and walked around him. 'This is no trick, I assure you!' he said to the shocked audience, as he used his fingers to feel the point of the sword between the performer's breast and naval. 'The man has indeed swallowed the sword!'

'Ask him to do it again!' someone from the crowd demanded, unable to believe that it was real.

The sword swallower obliged, performing the trick twice more to the satisfaction of the audience that watched mesmerized, stunned and speechless.

'This is fantastic!' a man in a brown suit jumped forward. 'Nothing like anything else I've seen before! I will give you 1000 pagodas,' he said, patting the performer on his back, 'if you will travel with me to Europe. And another 1000 for performances across England! It would be the most spectacular thing people have seen!'

'That is a kind offer!' Hannah whispered to her brother. Others in the audience clapped and cheered.

'Honestly,' the Englishman continued, 'people in Europe have seen magicians and jugglers and conjurers of all kinds. But this is most unique. They will be ready to pay an arm and a leg to watch this sort of thing! The exotic sword swallower of the Indies!'

'I'm sure that's more money than the poor fellow will see in his entire life!' Macaulay whispered back to his sister. 'Too good an offer to refuse!'

But the man on stage didn't seem as pleased. He stared blankly at the white sahib.

'I'll take care of everything. You have nothing to worry about!' the Englishman assured the man, pulling out some gold coins from his pocket as an advance to seal the deal.

'No, sahib!' the performer said humbly, pushing away the money. 'I cannot!'

'But why not? You would be famous!'

'You're never going to get an opportunity like this! You'd be a fool to refuse!' another voice in the crowd reasoned.

'Sahib . . . I am a Hindu,' said the sword-swallower, bowing to the Englishman with folded hands. 'I cannot cross the kala paani. If I cross the sea, I'd be contaminating my soul.'

'Bah!' Macaulay scoffed, getting up in a flash to leave the scene. 'Nonsense meets nonsense!'

As he tore off to the comfort of his study and the wisdom of Cicero, Macaulay was more convinced than ever before, that he had worked out the recipe India needed - Western thought and an English education.

Science had to take the place of dogma.

Sense had to prevail over nonsense.

5

WINDS OF CHANGE

Governor-General William Bentinck pulled his chair forward and examined the document that lay before him. The Minute, dated 2 February 1835, was submitted by Macaulay as President of the Committee of Public Instruction and ran into several pages. Bentinck drew himself closer to the light.

He knew he had placed his bets well. And yet, he found himself slightly apprehensive that morning. Princep had returned from his commission in Australia and there was always a threat he'd convert one of the pro-English members to his side. A swing in favour of the Orientalists at the eleventh hour was the last thing he wanted.

He began to read.

His eyes skimmed over the preliminaries as he searched for the words he wished to see. He paused at words and sentences that caught his attention, turning pages, nodding in agreement, even smiling when his eyes caught something that pleased him.

What then shall that language be?

One half of the committee maintain that it should be the English. The other half strongly recommend the Arabic and Sanskrit.

The whole question seems to me to be-which language is the best worth knowing?

I have no knowledge of either Sanskrit or Arabic. But I have done what I could to form a correct estimate of their value. I have read translations of the most celebrated Arabic and Sanskrit works . . .

A single shelf of a good European library was worth the whole native literature of India and Arabia.

It is, I believe, no exaggeration to say that all the historical information which has been collected from all the books written in the Sanskrit language is less valuable than what may be found in the most paltry abridgments used at preparatory schools in England.

Bentinck was pleased with what he had cursorily found in the early pages. He wished for this report to become the foundation for him to push his reforms through. It looked like it would meet his expectations after all. He continued to read.

The people of India do not require to be paid for eating rice when they are hungry, or for wearing woollen cloth in the cold season. To come nearer to the case before us: The children who learn their letters and a little elementary arithmetic from the village schoolmaster are not paid by him. He is paid for teaching them.

Why then is it necessary to pay people to learn Sanskrit and Arabic? Evidently, because it is universally felt that the Sanskrit and Arabic are languages, the knowledge of which does not compensate for the trouble of acquiring them. On all such subjects, the state of the market is the decisive test.

Bentinck mulled over those words. Yes, indeed. The market was the decisive test. Already, a number of boys were studying at the few private institutions in Calcutta teaching English and western sciences. Their families were paying the tutors, not demanding subsidies and scholarships from them. Macaulay had hit the nail on its head. The market was the ultimate test.

He returned to the report.

We must, at present, do our best to form a class who may be interpreters between us and the millions whom we govern, a class of persons Indian in blood and colour, but English in tastes, in opinions, in morals and in intellect.

Bentinck was pleased to read the report. There was, of course, one more objection. The fear amongst natives that western education was being brought in to convert Indians to Christianity, especially since many schools were set up by Christian missionaries. Macaulay suggested that they abstain from encouraging conversions. He concurred and returned to the report.

How then stands the case? We have to educate a people who cannot at present be educated by means of their mother tongue. We must teach them some foreign language . . .

. . . the English tongue is that which would be the most useful to our native subjects.

Bentinck threw his head back and rocked on his chair, feeling contented.

Macaulay had given him what he wanted.

English was the answer for India.

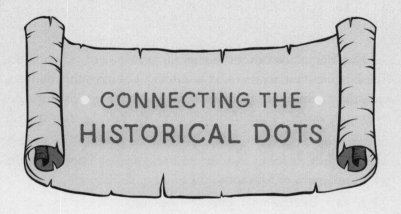

CONNECTING THE
HISTORICAL DOTS

 ### WHY DO YOU SPEAK ENGLISH FLUENTLY?

'. . . a class of persons Indian in blood and colour, but English in tastes, in opinions, in morals and in intellect.'

To create such a class was the intent of Bentinck, Macaulay and the British East India Company, when they brought about a policy change in 1835 to make English the medium of instruction for education in India.

Today, a large number of Indians are educated in English and speak it more fluently than their own mother tongue. The term 'Macaulay's children' is used to refer to this group—a pejorative term—meaning someone who went to an English-medium school and can read Shakespeare and Wordsworth but not their own native literature.

French children are taught French and official communication in France is in French. Japanese children are taught Japanese and all official communication in Japan is in that language.

But English is not an Indian language. And yet, it is the first language for many of us in India. It is also, for the large part, the medium of official communication in government.

One of the main reasons why we, as Indians, are able to read and speak English fluently—and are often more at ease with English than our own mother tongues—is because of the famous Minute of Macaulay, captured in this story.

In fact, increasingly, a number of Indians today are unable to speak their own native languages! Some even look down upon Indian languages and Indians who do not speak English.

Macaulay, in introducing English education, led to the creation of a new class of elite Indians, who were disconnected with their own country, people and languages. And the debate about the use, place and priority given to English in our education system still continues to this day.

The number of Indians who speak English has been growing over the years. Moreover, English is seen as a language that provides people with access to jobs all over the world. On the other hand, some Indian languages have been gradually going extinct.

Macaulay carried deep-rooted prejudice and racial bias when he came to India. Ask yourself if you carry Macaulay's bias? Do you consider English better than Indian languages? Do you consider yourself superior because you know how to speak, write and talk in English? Do you make fun of or look down upon those who can't? Why do you think this is so?

Give it some thought and you might discover something fascinating about your past, your present and yourself!

UNBOX THE PAST: LEARN HISTORY HIDDEN IN THE STORY.

 A PUSH FOR CHANGE

Around the 1820s, officials of the British East India Company, that ruled large parts of India, began to realize that without local support, it was difficult to run an efficient government. Hence, they wanted to hire local people. However, in order for them to do so, Indians would first need to be educated in a manner that could suit the Company's needs.

A Committee of Public Instruction was constituted in 1823 to develop facilities in India for education along western lines through the medium of the English language.

This committee comprised members of two groups: one called the Anglicists (Westernizers), who supported the use of the English language and Western sciences and ideas. Anglicists wanted to set up schools in India along the lines of the English public schools. The other group was called the Orientalists, who supported the use of vernacular Indian languages and wanted to revive classical learning in India.

The Anglicists argued that the point of education is to provide 'useful', or in other words, *European* knowledge. This was based on the ideas of James Mill, a leading English thinker of the time. Anglicists believed that India needed to undergo a change which could only come about on the basis of European values, literature and science.

The Orientalists too agreed that western education should to be introduced in India but the main difference was that they believed Western education must be taught in Indian languages. Some people saw the introduction of English as a promotion of Christianity and an attack on native Indian languages and traditions.

The story you just read is based on the conflict between these two groups.

 ## ORIENTALISTS' OUTLOOK

There were a handful of British officials posted in India who actually learnt Indian languages and read Indian literature. They looked at India with an open mind and were willing to learn about the country.

One of the most outstanding Orientalists was Sir William Jones who came to India in 1783 as a judge of the Supreme Court in Calcutta. He founded the Asiatic Society of Bengal in 1784 to encourage the study of India. He learned Sanskrit and declared that it was more perfect than Greek and Latin. He translated works of Sanskrit literature into English. His work led to various discoveries about India and its history, including the link between the languages of India and Europe.

James Princep is another Orientalist who greatly contributed to Indian Studies. It is due to his painstaking work that we know so much about Emperor Ashoka. Records about Ashoka had been completely lost until Princep decoded Brahmi, the script used for the inscriptions in the Ashokan pillars and edicts.

In fact, many Indian monuments were discovered, studied, recorded and restored due to the efforts of a number of Englishmen who took a keen interest in Indic studies. To them, we owe much of our knowledge of Indian history.

ENGLISH TO CUT COSTS!

Lord Warren Hastings, the earlier governor-general of India, spoke Urdu, Bengali and some Persian. He realized that in order for British rule in India to prosper, it was necessary for the British administrators to become familiar with Indian languages and customs. He believed that the government needed to work with the native institutions without trying to impose their own western ideas upon India.

However, in the 1830s, the East India Company was under pressure to reduce its administrative costs and better manage its finances. One of the ways of doing so was relying less on British officers and more on Indians to fill various judicial and administrative posts in India.

In order to do so, they needed to educate more Indians in English so that they could qualify themselves for the job. Further, it was cheaper to provide books in English than to translate them large scale into Indian languages, of which there were many.

This was one of the reasons that led to the introduction of English in India. And as we now know, a new class of Indians arose amongst the middle class in big cities that spoke fluent English and was highly westernized in their approach and thinking.

 ## PIONEER OF MODERN EDUCATION

One of the pioneers of western education in India and the use of English was Raja Ram Mohan Roy.

While the Anglicists and Orientalists clashed, Raja Ram Mohan Roy addressed a petition to Lord Amherst, the governor-general before Lord Bentinck, urging him to introduce western education in India based on the English model.

This petition is seen as one of the reasons schools in India were set up along the English model.

Some of the other major contributions of Raja Ram Mohan Roy were social reforms, including the abolition of Sati and setting up free regional languages press in India.

 ## A NEW CLASS OF INDIANS

After western education came to India, in the early 19th century, a new class of Indians arose. This was the middle class, who spoke English and were educated in government-aided schools where western concepts were taught. Bengal was the first place where this was established. Known as the Bengali Renaissance, it was spearheaded by reformers such as Raja Ram Mohan Roy, who were of the view that European knowledge was needed to uplift Indians.

English gradually began to be seen as the key that opened the door to better jobs. Over time, English-educated Indians began to favour English over their own languages. In fact, when Lord Mayo and, thereafter, Lord Curzon tried to bring in vernacular primary education, it was the English-educated Indians who opposed them. Some of them even referred to the thought of giving up English as committing 'intellectual suicide'.

Over a period of time, however, Indian leaders began to object to this policy. Many, such as Tagore and Gandhi, argued that a child learnt best in his/her own mother tongue. Some of them argued that an English education was giving birth to a new class of elite Indians, many of whom were incapable of expressing themselves in any Indian language.

The impact of this policy and these movements can be felt in India to this day.

 ## MACAULAY'S MINUTE

The official introduction of English education in India took place by an order dated 7 March 1835, issued by Governor-General William Bentinck after going through a document (the Minute) written by Thomas Macaulay, dated 2 February 1835. Parts of this Minute are captured in the story.

The long Minute drawn up by Macaulay put forward the following recommendations:

(1) English should replace Persian as the official language;

(2) English ought to be introduced as the medium of instruction in all institutions of learning.

These recommendations were made on the basis of Macaulay's belief that English was the language that had '*ready access to all the vast intellectual wealth*' of the wisest nations of the earth over several generations.

 ## MACAULAY, THE MAN

Thomas Babington Macaulay came to India in June 1834 as a member of the Supreme Council of India.

He stayed on in India for four years before returning to England. During this period, he did two things that left an imprint on India for generations to come:

1. Westernization of India's education policy and the introduction of English in schools and colleges in India;

2. Drafting the Indian Penal Code.

Macaulay's views of India were typical of Englishmen of that period, who based their thinking on *The History of British India* by James Mill. Mill had never visited India, nor did he speak any Indian language. Yet, the book written by him about India was essential reading for all Englishmen coming to work in India!

Most Englishman of that period considered Britain to be a civilizing influence on India and Macaulay was no exception.

STORIES OF
CREATIVITY
AND
ENTERPRISE

THE SCULPTOR OF MAHABALIPURAM

1

BREATHING LIFE INTO STONE

'Aiya . . . may I join you when you visit the Kanchi Fort?' Shekhar asked his guru nervously.

Surprised by the request, Vidyadhara, master sculptor of the Pallavas, turned towards his disciple, eyebrow raised.

Kal! Kal! Kal! The sound of hammer on chisel could be heard from all directions. Sculptors and their assistants were busy carving figures of gods and goddesses, humans and animals out of huge blocks of granite hewn out of the rock-front of the hill. In the distance, white waves crashed on to the shore of Mamallapuram.

'Shekhara! You are a young apprentice. You joined me less than a year ago, didn't you?' asked Vidyadhara, candidly.

Shekhar looked down, disappointed. The dream of meeting the Pallava emperor was surely too big for a novice like him. Sure, he had worked very hard over the past year and had sculpted some exceedingly fine pieces. The sculpture of Shiva he had made last month had left everyone spellbound. The proportions had been perfect. The tension of the muscles and the grace of the bodily movement, lifelike. The statue's expression had been divine. Few had believed it was the work of an amateur sculptor. 'The grace of god shone upon young Shekhar,' craftsmen had whispered to one another. His teacher too had been left awestruck. But he was young. Perhaps, he had overstepped his position by dreaming of going to the Kanchi Fort to meet Emperor Mahendravarman.

Vidyadhara stepped closer to Shekhar and put his arm on his student's shoulder. 'I often visit Kanchi to meet the emperor to apprise him of the work. But never before has a student made a request to join me for my meeting with the king!' he said, his expression serious.

Shekhar's face fell. He cursed himself for having asked the question, and nervously scratched the scar on his right arm. He didn't want to fall out of his guru's favour.

'You have asked for the impossible! But I am pleased by your boldness. Your dedication and skills have impressed me!' Vidyadhara continued after a brief pause. 'Not only are you a good student and a wonderful sculptor but also a man who dares to take initiative. Yes, you can certainly join me!' laughed Vidyadhara, finally ending the suspense and patting Shekhar's back.

Shekhar fell at his master's feet and held on to his ankles. 'Thank you Aiya. I will not forget this day till my death.'

'Never mind all that!' replied Vidyadhara. 'Now hurry up and get ready. You can't show up before the Pallavendra with tattered, mud-stained clothes. He's the Lord of the Pallavas, after all! Put on something decent! Hurry up . . . get going!'

As Shekhar ran towards the shed, which he shared with a dozen other aspiring sculptors, Vidyadhara looked around at the site as he gathered his manuscripts with drawings and proposals for further work. In a little over a year, the barren hillside of Kadal Malai had turned into a busy quarry and sculpting haven. The vision of Chakravarti Mahendravarman

Pallava of building a lasting legacy in stone was slowly bearing fruit. Vidyadhara smiled with satisfaction, watching the vast expanse before him, dotted with a thousand crouching sculptors working the stone. Kings waged wars. Emperors enlarged empires. But the Pallava king spent his time composing music and writing plays, sculpting stone and painting murals.

'Vidyadhara, one day, I will be gone and so will this empire,' Mahendravarman had said to him once, many years ago. 'But our legacy in stone will outlive us all. Generations to come will see these beautifully sculpted figures on the shores of Mamallapuram and remember that a king once walked the land who cared more for art than war.'

Vidyadhara had bowed his head in submission. He considered himself fortunate to have been born in the land of a king who placed art above all else.

And thus began the vision of the Shore temple of Mamallapuram. Lost in these thoughts, Vidyadhara collected his manuscripts and climbed up on the bullock cart that was waiting to take him to the riverfront so he could make his way to Kanchi. The king's messenger who had brought the summons for the master sculptor to present himself immediately at Kanchi, stood by on his horse.

'Aiya! Wait up!' Shekhar, dressed in a bright yellow tunic, ran towards the bullock cart as it was making its way out.

'Shekhara! Come!' Vidyadhara extended his hand out to his disciple, as Shekhar jumped into the moving cart.

'Show this . . . to the guards at the fort gates,' the king's messenger said to Vidyadhara handing him a scroll stamped with the royal insignia.

'What is this, Anna? What need do I have for this? Have I not visited the Pallavendra several times before?'

'That may be so,' replied the messenger. 'But times have changed. The fort is heavily guarded now. You will not be allowed to enter without this,' he said and galloped away.

Puzzled, Vidyadhara looked down at the scroll in his hand. What was the meaning of this? The master sculptor of the Pallava Empire would not be allowed inside the Kanchi Fort without sanction? He felt insulted. But he was also confused. What great emergency could have arisen that the king had summoned him immediately to the fort? And why was the fort heavily guarded? Vidyadhara was filled with a deep sense of foreboding as he surveyed the hundreds of craftsmen and sculptors chipping away with hammers and chisels on the mountainside, breathing life into stone.

2

AT THE THRESHOLD

Awestruck, Shekhar gazed at the rising walls of the Kanchi Fort as their cart neared the city. For decades, he had heard about this great centre of learning but had never quite imagined that someday he'd be within its towering walls. The winding highway forked into two as it neared the fort and Shekhar could feel his pulse racing.

It was nearing evening and the sun was about to dip behind the ramparts. The imposing southern gateway of the fort loomed high before them. A steady stream of people made their way out of the wooden gate, secured with heavy iron chains and a huge metal bolt. Drums began to be beaten to signal the closure of the gates for the day as birds nesting in the crevices of the walls flew out in alarm.

Vidyadhara surveyed the soldiers standing at the gates with spears in their hands, swords on their waists and horns around their necks. The fort appeared more heavily guarded than usual.

'The master sculptor is here. Allow him through,' announced a guard, who recognized Vidyadhara as they approached.

'You know the orders,' said another turning to him sternly. 'Nobody without authorization is to be permitted.'

Vidyadhara did not want an altercation. He produced the missive he had received, stamped with the royal insignia. The guard scrutinized it under an illuminated torchlight and nodded. A horn was sounded out to alert the other guard to open the gate.

The small door in the gate led to the fort through a narrow wooden bridge over a moat that was filled with blue-green water. The clicking of bolts and iron chains was once again heard, as a guard at the other end of the moat bridge opened another gate, letting the two sculptors through.

Vidyadhara was annoyed. Shekhar was astounded.

'You guards are doing such a fabulous job!' remarked Shekhar. 'The fort is said to be impenetrable because of your valued service.' Flattered, the guard smiled.

'But this gate . . . it is wide enough only for a small bullock cart. How do large chariots and elephants enter the fort, Aiya?' asked Shekhar.

'Well, the gates at the north and the east are wide. Even elephants can walk through them,' replied the guard.

Stepping inside the hallowed precincts of the fort, Shekhar spun around to soak in the views from all sides. He noticed a platoon of guards standing at the upper storey of the gate watching the horizon at a distance. On the west, he noticed rows of horses neighing and hundreds of soldiers milling around in the distance. Wherever he looked, he saw wide avenues leading to street corners marked with pillars upon which were placed large burning torches. Flags bearing the Rishabha, the bull insignia of the Pallavas, fluttered everywhere as a great din caused by hundreds of soldiers, horses and elephants could be heard rising

from a distance. As they turned another corner, they noticed cart loads of drums, conches and bugles being moved towards the gate. It was obvious that something unusual was going on.

Vidyadhara looked out towards the towers of the Ekambareshwar Temple in the distance.

'Hara Hara!' he muttered. 'May the blessings of Lord Shiva forever grace Kanchi.'

Shekhar looked around at the dozens of temple towers in the city asking Vidyadhara to name them, as their cart slowly wound its way up towards the palace. Turning the next corner, Vidyadhara told Shekhar about the bustling market place he would soon see, where he could buy anything from grains to gems. But to their surprise, he found the market closed. In its place, were dozens of smithies with blacksmiths who were occupied making spears and swords.

'This is unbelievable!' exclaimed Shekhar. 'Is the fort always like this?'

'It has never been this way,' Vidyadhara shook his head in puzzlement. 'I wonder what the matter is!' he said, with a worried look on his face. Then, noticing that Shekhar was scribbling away furiously on a bunch of palm leaves, he asked, 'What are you writing?'

'Sir, my dear old mother in the village has dreamed of visiting this great centre of learning, where scholars from Taxila to Kanyakumari flock. But she has never had the opportunity to do so. And perhaps she will never get a chance to see the fort. As an artist, I thought perhaps I could show her some drawings and impressions of the fort. So that she may see through my eyes.'

Vidyadhara nodded and smiled. He was glad he had Shekhar for company. An overwhelming sense of foreboding was taking a grip of his senses. As they reached the palace gates, he noticed, to his surprise, the crown prince, Mammallar, dismounting his steed.

'Here comes the master sculptor of the Pallava kingdom. Welcome!' exclaimed the Pallava prince, as he patted his horse to be sent away to the royal stables. Vidyadhara couldn't help noting that the prince was not dressed in his resplendent silks and pearls as he usually was at this hour. Instead, he was in battle gear, covered from neck to toe in his armour.

'Mammallar! It is always a delight to come here and meet you and the Pallavendra. But today, after seeing the fort like this, I am restless,' said Vidyadhara.

'Come. Let's go inside and talk. Father is waiting for you,' said the prince, leading the way into the palace.

As they made their way in, Shekhar could hear his heart beating wildly. He could scarce believe he was walking right behind Mammallar, the mighty wrestler, and was about to have an audience with the emperor himself. Shekhar soaked in the striking impressions on the walls which were adorned with paintings of Lord Shiva in all his majestic forms as he walked along the labyrinth of hallways. Never before had he witnessed such majesty and splendour.

'These paintings! Has the king made them all?' Shekhar whispered to his guru, as they walked along.

'But of course! The king is not called Chitrakara Puli for nothing!' Vidyadhara beamed, surveying the murals. 'He is indeed the tiger amongst painters.'

Shekhar moved closer. The details in the fine paintings mesmerized him. The artist in him rejoiced at seeing such beauty. He stopped to notice the brush strokes, tried to understand how the paint had been mixed.

'The king is waiting in the veranda upstairs,' a guard told them, as Mammallar and Vidyadhara proceeded towards the stairway.

Lost in the paintings, Shekhar did not hear those words. And thus began the terrific adventure of the night.

3

A ROYAL ENCOUNTER

Vidyadhara felt reassured when he saw the Emperor taking a stroll in the broad leafy veranda above the courtyard. The king was safe and his demeanour composed. Dressed in royal silks with a striking blue *angavastram* covering his torso, adorned with *navaratna* necklaces and his famed crown of gold, the Pallavendra appeared in control of the situation. But he looked deep in thought.

'Vidya!' the emperor exclaimed when he saw the master sculptor. 'I cannot tell you how happy I am to see you.'

Vidyadhara was about to prostrate before the king but the Chakravarthi lifted him up by his shoulders.

'You have travelled a long way, Vidya. You must be tired. I would have offered that you rest before we talk, but unfortunately today, I do not have the luxury of time. We must talk immediately.'

'What is the matter Chakravarthi? You seem disturbed. And everything in the fort . . . it is . . . so . . . so charged up and different.'

'Yes . . . I am about to leave for the battlefront, Vidya. But I had to speak to you before leaving.'

'Battlefront!' exclaimed Vidyadhara. 'Prabhu! I realized something was amiss as I entered the fort. But hearing it from you is deeply disconcerting.'

The emperor smiled. 'Artists are made for higher purposes. I am not surprised you did not know about the war till you entered the gates of Kanchi!'

'Pardon my ignorance, Prabhu! Nothing except the sound of hammer upon chisel reaches my ears.'

'You are a fortunate man, Vidya!' laughed the emperor. 'I wish I had a life devoted to art like yours. Alas, as king I must tear away from what I love most and attend to other worldly affairs.'

Vidyadhara turned back to introduce his young disciple to the king. But Shekhar was not there! Vidyadhara spun around to look for his pupil. But he was missing. The master sculptor was puzzled but the king soon broached a serious topic and there was no time to think of other matters.

'Vidyadhara, I have called you here for an important reason. You know the Mamallapuram project is a dream. It is a dream we have both visualized together. But now, with this war looming, I am afraid the work must be halted.' Mahendravarman paused for Vidyadhara to absorb the full import of his words. The sculptor stared at the king, his face expressionless.

'Vidya . . . I cannot say what will happen. I, much less our astrologers, cannot accurately predict the outcome of this war. But if I do not return . . .'

'Appa! Please don't talk like that,' Mammallar interjected sharply.

'Very well . . . let me rephrase my sentence,' nodded the king, throwing a gentle look at his son.

'Pulakesin, the Chalukya king, is charging towards us with an army . . . mightier than we can muster. Taking advantage of the situation, Durveenitha, the Ganga king is charging at us from the west. The resources we have need to be funnelled towards fighting this war, Vidya. The sculpting project that we both dreamed of, I am afraid it will remain a dream for now.'

'Prabhu! I don't know what to say,' said Vidyadhara.

'This decision has not been easy for me to take, Vidya. I worship my art. It is my tribute to the divine. But I am compelled to take this decision as king. It is in the best interests of this kingdom. I have to give this war all I've got.'

'I pray that you return victorious from the battlefield, Prabhu. Until then, it will be as you command,' said Vidyadhara, trying hard to ignore his disappointment.

'You will have to convey this to all your craftsmen,' said the king. 'They can move further south to Chola Nadu till things settle down if they so desire,' the king continued.

'Do not worry about that, O King,' replied Vidyadhara. 'I will manage that. Oblivious to the events, I brought you this tube containing a palm leaf manuscript of the drawings for the proposed sculptures. But I suppose this has no meaning any more,' said Vidyadhara softly, with downcast eyes.

'Don't lose heart, Vidya. The work will resume soon. Give me the manuscript. I am eager to see your designs and take stock of the progress. We will resume soon. I assure you.'

The sound of drums arose in the distance. Trumpets began to blare. Vidyadhara was alarmed. Was the army beginning its forward march? But why would it set out in the darkness of the night, he wondered.

'Alert! Beware! A spy from the Vatapi Army is inside the Kanchi Fort. A Chalukyan spy is inside Kanchi!' an announcer proclaimed between drumbeats.

Two officers came rushing in to meet the king.

'Chakravarti! A Vatapi spy of the Chalukyan king has been found in the fort. All gates have been shut and secured! We will nab the scoundrel!'

The king frowned and crossed his hands behind him. It wasn't a good sign.

Vidyadhara turned to leave. The king had more pressing matters to attend to. He turned to look for Shekhar again. The boy was still missing. He couldn't understand. The lad was so excited to meet the Pallavendra and had vanished just at the moment their meeting began!

'What news?' Mahendra Pallava demanded from Murugappa, the chief of security at the fort, who came panting down the veranda.

'We have definite news that a spy has entered the Kanchi Fort,' Murugappa gasped. 'A tall and broad-shouldered bloke with a scar on his forearm. He was seen with tubes of manuscripts that contained detailed drawings of the fort. He was wearing a turmeric coloured upper garment and sported short curly hair.'

Vidyadhara was about to descend the flight of stairs after taking the king's leave when he heard those words. His eyes grew wide in horror. The import of Shekhar's sudden disappearance struck him like a thunderbolt.

'Appa, excuse me so I may immediately attend to this emergency,' Mammalar requested his father before quickly disappearing into the hallway. The king began discussing something with Murugappa.

Vidyadhara's throat went dry. The pieces of the puzzle were beginning to fall into place. Shekhar's insistence on coming to the fort, drawing the map of Kanchi for his ailing mother, his enquires about which gates were wide enough to allow chariots and elephants to come through, asking Vidyadhara to point out the landmarks of the city, his sudden absence—they were all beginning to connect.

And yet, a voice inside him refused to believe it. It refused to accept that he, the master sculptor of the Pallava kingdom, had been the gate pass that enabled an enemy spy to enter the impenetrable gates of the Kanchi Fort. How had he made such a blunder? How could he have allowed a young lad to fool him like this? Oh Lord! How was he to make up for this mistake?

There was no reprieve. He had to inform the king and provide the guards with all the information and support he could offer.

'Alert! Beware! A Vatapi spy in a yellow tunic and a scar on his forearm is in Kanchi Fort. We must nab him before he gets away!' A guard called out in the distance, as similar announcements tore through the night air all across the city.

Vidyadhara slowly approached the king, his eyes brimming with tears, his voice quaking.

It was going to be a long eventful night.

4

A SPY ON THE LOOSE

As the king left and his officers scurried away to attend to the emergency, Vidyadhara closed his eyes to pray. He had never wished ill upon this kingdom. Always worked and prayed for its prosperity and glory. But perhaps now, he was going to be an instrument in its downfall.

'The Chakravarti has ordered that the fort be prepared for a siege. We are to stock up on provisions for the fort to withstand a two-year siege,' voices of officials and palace staff could be heard from the courtyard below.

'Those who need not stay within are to be evacuated. Those outside who need to be safeguarded are to be brought within the fort. Or directed to leave for Chola Nadu till the end of the war,' another voice drifted up to the veranda above.

Vidyadhara's thoughts raced. He remembered Shekhar's questions to the security about the gates through which elephants and cart traffic could enter. He recalled Shekhar making drawings of the fort as they made their way in, supposedly to show his mother. Vidyadhara kicked himself. How had he been so foolish?

Unknowingly, he had also become a traitor by allowing a spy to enter. He felt miserable.

'Do you know the Vatapi army plans on feeding its elephants liquor and allowing them to run amok in Kanchi? They think they can tear down the gates of the fort like that!' another man in the courtyard below laughed.

'Aiya, have you heard nothing about the ocean-like Chalukyan army advancing towards the Pallava kingdom? They have crossed the Tungabhadra and have entered Pallava-nadu. They have over 10,000 horsemen and more than a 1000 elephants. Not to mention lakhs of foot soldiers. That is the strength of their army. You'd be a fool to think we stand any chance against them!' came the reply.

Perspiration dotted Vidyadhara's brow as he paced up and down the veranda. His heart was beating faster. He imagined Shekhar trying to get out of the fort. He wished that the boy would fall into the massive moat in the darkness. He imagined Shekhar flying past the soldiers on a horse. *Does he know how to ride a horse*, Vidyadhara wondered. Perhaps he does, given he is a spy. How the boy had tricked him into believing he was a sculpting student. Perhaps two *jammams* had passed after sunset. There was still no news. He felt helpless.

'This is what happens when the king wastes his time with music and art instead of investing his efforts in warfare!' he heard another man trying to whisper, although the breeze carried his voice to the upper storey.

'Even Lord Shiva cannot protect the fort if the Vatapi Army marches here!'

'Shhh . . . Don't say that. You will dishearten the soldiers. Don't you know that, at the crack of dawn tomorrow, our army marches out into the battlefield? Our king can win this war using his intelligence, even though might is with the other side.'

'Intelligence!' laughed another, spitting on the ground with contempt. 'An enemy spy has entered the Kanchi Fort. If he escapes, Pulakesin will be have the details of the fort a mere two days from now. Our army will be decimated and the Vatapi king will be marching into Kanchi next month.'

'Don't say such things! I have told you so many times not to say inauspicious things!'

'How does my saying or not saying something change matters? Our king is busy writing poetry and sculpting stone. Like his master sculptor here who is so lost, he didn't know of the impending war. Worse, he allows a spy into the fort!'

Vidyadhara held his head in his hands and sunk to the floor, distraught at what he was hearing. 'Oh, Lord Shanmugha! Will the Kaveri not consume me in her waters? I only wished to bring glory and fame to the king and this kingdom. And now I have brought nothing but ill-luck upon them!' He wished he could turn back time and overturn his decision of accepting Shekhar into his fold.

The gates at the other end of the courtyard below opened and a group of people could be seen approaching. Vidyadhara strained his eyes to see. Mammallar could be seen walking ahead with Murugappa and some other officials and ministers. Walking behind them was the emperor with a big smile, patting the back of a tall boy who walked alongside him.

Vidyadhara's eyes grew wide in disbelief as the party neared the torchlight inside the courtyard.

The emperor was walking with none other than Shekhar!

5

A MATTER OF SURVIVAL

'Vidya!' the voice of the Pallavendra called out to him. Tears streaming down his cheeks, Vidyadhara fell at the king's feet.

'Pardon me, Pallavendra! Pardon this poor wretched soul. I know not how I made this blunder of failing to recognize that traitor!'

'Vidya, you have given me a saviour. Your disciple has . . .'

Sobbing, Vidyadhara stood up to face the king. A beaming Shekhar was standing beside him.

'You scoundrel! You traitor! You betrayer!' exclaimed Vidyadhara, as he started to beat his disciple.

Mammallar stood in the way to block his blows upon the boy. 'Vidya! Stop!' Mahendravarman pulled the boy back.

'The boy has helped us catch the spy! He is *not* the spy!'

Vidyadhara froze in the midst of thrashing his student. 'Prabhu! What did you say?'

'The boy has helped us catch the spy. He is *not* the spy!' Mammallar repeated his father's words.

'Shekhara! Is this true?' Vidyadhara asked his disciple, now lying on the floor, rubbing his sore back.

'Tell your guru, Shekhara! Tell him what a fine job you have done in saving the kingdom,' said the emperor.

Shekhar stood up hesitantly, still fearing that more blows from his guru's hands might rain down on him. 'As we were entering the palace,' he began, 'I was staring at the beautiful paintings and murals on the walls and got lost in the maze of corridors. When I tried to find my way back to you, I noticed a shadow lurking in the distance. I thought it might be a guard and I was scared I'd be asked to leave the palace. Hence, I hid behind a pillar. That is when I realized the shadow was a spy.'

'How did you know he was a Vatapi spy?' Mammallar asked the boy.

'His behaviour seemed strange at first,' replied the sculptor. 'He was walking mysteriously in and out of the rooms in the long corridor. His eyes kept darting about as if they were looking for something. He didn't appear like a guard on duty or anybody legitimate in the palace.'

'And so, you followed him?'

'Yes! I felt compelled to keep track of him. Winding through doorways and verandas, I found he had made his way out and proceeded towards the royal stables behind the palace. There, he spoke to his accomplice hiding behind the murunga tree. And I understood immediately he was a spy.'

'What did he say?'

'It is not what he said that alerted me. But how he said it. He spoke in Telugu, not Tamil. My mother comes from the Siddhar Mountains in the north, and hence, I understand perfectly the language of the Chalukyans. He was telling his accomplice that he had the map of the palace and fort and now needed a horse to get away. They both decided to steal a horse.'

'And your disciple quickly alerted the sentries,' said Murugappa to Vidyadhara. 'Had it not been for his alertness, the spy may have slipped away. Immediate messages were sent out all across the fort and the security caught up with the fellow's horse just as he was about to exit the gates!'

'We must enquire into how such a breach of security occurred in the first place,' Mammalar remarked, shaking his head.

'Certainly!' Murugappa nodded.

'The Pallava kingdom is proud to have a citizen like you!' Mahendravarman proclaimed, patting Shekhar's back. Shekhar was blushing. He had never imagined his visit to Kanchi Fort would turn into such an adventure.

'Vidyadhara! I must borrow your disciple for a few months. This lad will be more useful to me at the battlefront than he is at the quarry.'

'He is a brilliant sculptor, Prabhu!' Vidyadhara began, eager to make amends for his earlier blunder.

'I have no doubt he is! And with a master like you, he can only get better. The gems of his hands will dazzle the world hundreds of years from today. But for the moment, we are fighting a battle to survive. I need him at the battlefront.'

The emperor turned to Shekhar. 'Will you work as my informant? The empire needs people like you, who are alert, agile and can speak the enemy language.'

Shekhar was speechless. Tears filled his eyes. His heart swelled with pride. He had never imagined being of use to king and kingdom. He turned towards his guru.

'Shekhara! Son, I know nothing about warfare and espionage. Don't look to me for guidance. The king is the best judge.'

'The Pallava country needs you my boy!' said Mahendravarman.

Shekhar nodded and fell at the feet of his guru and king.

'Murugappa! Take the boy into your fold and train him. He reports to you. His first task will be to discreetly befriend the Vatapi spy and extract information out of him,' instructed the Emperor.

'Rise, Shekhara! You have saved the kingdom from grave danger today. Your name shall forever be remembered. I am ashamed for having judged you wrongly. You have more important tasks at hand. May you all return victorious,' Vidyadhara blessed his disciple.

'I hate to tear an artist away from his labour of love,' said the Pallavendra turning to Vidyadhara. 'To me, there is no glory higher than art. No joy more divine.'

The king sighed to take a pause as he reflected upon his words.

'But when survival is at stake, nothing else matters!'

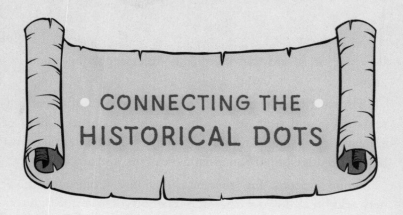

CONNECTING THE HISTORICAL DOTS

 CREATIVITY AND CONFLICT

Is conflict good or bad for creativity?

While this question appears in the story at a large-scale, it may also arise at a personal level.

When you are in the midst of a conflict with your friends, family or even your internal self and going through anxiety, stress or depression—is that when you are least creative or is that when you are most expressive?

Different theories exist regarding this. Conventional thinking says that conflict harms creativity. But conflict has also been seen as a force that makes people more determined to overcome challenges and work towards achieving the goal with greater perseverance.

Conflict has also led to growth and innovation. In science, a crisis is essential for a species to adapt, to evolve and to grow.

Likewise, it is said that conflict is necessary to help cultures grow.

Creativity can be defined as 'the achievement of something remarkable and new, something which transforms a field of endeavour in a significant way'. Usually, war and internal unrest have a negative impact on artistic creativity and artists.

Some reasons for that are obvious. Communications networks break down during war or periods of unrest. Resources are limited. Artists are unable to get the required resources/manpower to create. Administration is compelled to divert scarce resources towards fighting the war instead of pursuing creative goals (as in the story).

On the other hand, as you will no doubt have noticed, war and conflict have been the motif of many a literary work, as it forms a very dramatic background for expression. Let's take the example of India's freedom struggle. Literature and poetry thrived during the period. Nobel Laureate Rabindranath Tagore, Subramaniya Bharatiar, Shakuntala Devi, Ramdhari Singh Dinkar, Subhadra Kumari Chauhan, Mohamad Allama Iqbal and many others were inspired by the conflict to write great works of literature. Playwrights, artists, painters—many creative people were inspired by the struggle.

Several great works of Indian architecture were commissioned by kings from the spoils of war. World War I and II led to great advancement in science and technology.

Look around you. Who are the most creative people you know? How do you think conflict has influenced their creativity? Select a group of ten such people and make your observations. Do you find a pattern? Can you make any conclusions based on your observations?

UNBOX THE PAST: DISCOVER HISTORY HIDDEN IN THE STORY.

 RIDDLE OF THE SANDS

One of the greatest wonders of the marvellous monuments of Mahabalipuram is that they are all incomplete. Without exception, all the monuments at the site are unfinished. A few monuments like the Ganesha ratha are almost complete while others are barely begun. Scholars have for long contemplated and studied this phenomenon and wondered why. Why did the patrons and the artists, who worked so hard to carve out such beautiful forms out of hard granite, leave them incomplete? Mysteries like these, cause one to reflect upon whether war could have been a reason. The unfinished nature of the monuments hint at an abrupt cessation of the work.

 AN ARTIST KING

The work of sculpture at Mahabalipuram has been largely attributed to Mahendravarman, who ruled from AD 571 to 630. The monuments of this period reflect a greater sense of art and aesthetics. Usually, kings who patronized art funnelled resources towards the work. Rarely did they involve themselves in its creation. That was left to the artists.

Mahendravarman was known to be a great artist himself. The titles he has been given reflect that—Vidhi (creator), Vichitracitta (the curious minded) and Matta-vilasa (drunk with pleasure). He was also a gifted musician and composer. He wrote great poetry and dramas, including the Matta Vilasa and the *Bhagavadajjuka*, a great comedy of errors.

Scholars believe that the artistic genius and eccentricity of Mahendravarman Pallava is behind what is considered to be India's most original and aesthetically superb group of monuments.

 ## DUTY OF A RULER

Had Mahendravarman focussed on military might instead of artistic endeavours, do you think he may have safeguarded his kingdom? What, in your opinion, is the primary duty of a ruler? The safety of his kingdom and people? Or the pursuit of knowledge and arts?

How many kings and political leaders do you know who are also artists? If we had artists and creative people for rulers, do you think this world might have been a more peaceful place or would it have been chaotic?

 ## COMPLETING THE HISTORY PUZZLE

Why are the monuments in Mahabalipuram incomplete?

When presented with a question such as this, how does one find the answer? The work of the historian is to piece together the puzzle, despite the missing pieces. The joy of discovering history, is partly in understanding these gaps and imagining what might have filled them.

Faced with such a situation, historians turn to various kinds of evidence to arrive at the truth. There could be archaeological evidence, such as the monuments themselves, the style of construction and dating the material used. There are literary evidences such as records of travellers like the Chinese traveller Hiuen Tsang who visited Kanchi and left records of his voyages.

However, we generally find limited literary evidence about Indian history.

There are also epigraphic sources which are the inscriptions that one finds at a site. And with these tools, historians must use their imagination to piece together the puzzle. Perhaps you can use your imagination to try and find an answer to why these Pallava masterpieces were left unfinished. You might arrive at a unique answer.

 ## GENIUS OF CRAFTSMANSHIP

There are two kinds of rock temples you will find in India. One is the rock-cut monolith which is cut into the face of a hill. This kind of temple is created by chipping away the stone from the hill. The other type is a structural stone temple, which is built with stone that is mined from a stone quarry and carried to the site for construction.

All the monuments at Mahabalipuram are monolithic, i.e., they have been carved out of a stone hill. Sculptors and workers worked with only hammer and chisel, and patiently chipped away tons of hard granite, moulding it into beautiful forms.

Unlike in the west, where the works of great artists like Michelangelo and Da Vinci are acknowledged by name, rarely do we find names of Indian sculptors and artists mentioned with their works. This is perhaps because art was seen as a service to the gods and the artist wished to remain anonymous. Or perhaps patrons and kings wished only their names to be known. Or perhaps, it could have been that records of their names are lost. Either way, we do not know the names of those who worked tirelessly on these monuments that are a lasting legacy of India's architectural and artistic genius.

 ## CONFLICT AND ART

One of Picasso's most famous works is Guernica, which was inspired by conflict. In 1937, when he was looking for a subject to paint for the World Fair in Paris, he was so moved by the devastation caused by air strikes on a Spanish village called Guernica, that he chose it as a subject for his painting. The Spanish dictator, General Franco had allied with the Germans in war and permitted Hitler to carry out test strikes in Spain. About 1600 people were wounded or killed during the strikes. This painting became one of the most dramatic voices of protest against the war.

 ## WAR AND LITERATURE

War is a dramatic event that has inspired poets and writers across time in every part of the world. Some of the greatest works of literature have been inspired by wars or contain war as a central theme. The Ramayana, the Mahabharata, the Iliad and several other works are centred around epic wars. In modern times, Leo Tolstoy's *War and Peace* is a landmark work inspired by war.

 ## CONFLICT AND TECHNOLOGY

Conflict and war have caused large-scale damage and destruction. At the same time, they have given rise to some of the most revolutionary ideas and technologies. World War II gave rise to superior technology in the fields of communication, aviation, navigation and more. Find out more about how World War II impacted the technology we use today!

 ## MAHABALIPURAM

The ancient site on which these monuments were built was called Mallai (in Tamil, mallai means mountain) or Kadalmallai (in Tamil, kadal means the sea). This was a great port of the Pallava empire. The place was later named Mamallapuram in honour of Narasimha Varman, the son of Mahendravarman. He was given the title Mammallar, meaning 'Great Wrestler' since he was known to be an excellent wrestler and warrior.

THE TEA THIEF OF SCOTLAND

1

BANKIPUR

'You are turning us all into murderers!' alleged Kanjilal forcefully, compelling Jenkins to look up from the papers on his desk. 'We do not want our hands tainted by murder, sir!'

Despite the conditions, Jenkins couldn't help marvelling at the man's audacity. It took some guts for an Indian peasant to march up to an English sahib of the East India Company, look him in the eye and assert himself boldly this way.

'Please understand, sir,' Kanjilal continued, turning to a more conciliatory tone. 'My fertile land is being turned into a wasteland. For generations, my forefathers have grown millets and vegetables on this land, which has fed not just my own family but many others too. Your policy is wreaking havoc upon me and other farmers of the region.'

Jenkins leaned forward on his desk casually and looked straight into the eyes of the petitioner. Dressed in a dull white dhoti-kurta with a grey overcoat and a traditional rectangular cap over his head, Kanjilal, Jenkins reckoned, was more than a poor peasant.

He had that air about him. Ten other men stood submissively behind Kanjilal with folded hands, joining in his request.

'The officers of the East India Company have forced us to plant poppy seeds in place of our regular crops. Opium does not feed our children, sir,' he cried. 'Opium is of little use. And they're saying . . . Opium is killing thousands in China.'

Jenkins did not react. Yes, it was true. The last he had heard, over a million people in China were addicted to the drug. He turned to look out at the factory floor, averting his gaze from the farmer. Thousands of cakes of crude opium lay piled up. In the stacking room at the far end, raw opium was being refined by an army of workers, who were shaping it into balls and wrapping them into steamed poppy petals. From there, it found itself packed into chests to make way for Calcutta, where it would be sold at an auction to private shipping companies. Thereafter, it would leave for its final destination—China.

'Our hands are tainted with the blood of our dying brothers in China,' Kanjilal continued his supplications. 'Please, sir . . . we wish to grow millets and vegetables on our lands, as we did before!'

Jenkins let out a sigh. It was a new posting for the young asst. sub deputy of the Company. He was moved by Kanjilal's persuasive arguments. But his job required him to keep a steady supply of opium from the villages around Patna to the processing factories of the East India Company at Bankipur. He had to find a way to dismiss the persistent man.

'We will look into your petition,' said Jenkins, getting up from his desk and leading the men towards the door. 'We will let you know.'

'That is very kind of you, sir,' Kanjilal and the others bowed before him with folded hands. 'May God bless you for your kindness!'

As Kanjilal made his way out with the other peasants, cartloads of earthenware jars filled with opium trundled past them into the factory courtyard.

'Do you know,' said Banarsidas, 'I've heard that though they buy the opium from us at Rs 5 a *seer*, they sell it in China for many times that price?'

'We get virtually nothing for our toil and blood. Our backs break harvesting and processing all that poppy!' another said, shaking his head.

'Not to mention, turning in our land for growing this wretched crop,' quipped another.

Kanjilal looked heavenward. 'This sahib seems like a good man,' he said. 'Let's hope our prayers are answered.'

2

CALCUTTA

'You ought to know better than to ask me such a question!' remarked Hopkins, the sub deputy officer of the British East India Company, as he oversaw the loading of boxes of opium on ox-carts after the auction had been completed at the Company's office in Calcutta. Looking at the scene before him, Hopkins was rather pleased. The demand for opium seemed to have risen. He could report higher profits to London this cycle; his superiors would be pleased!

'I do understand,' mumbled Jenkins, following his superior. 'I do. But . . .'

'The East India Company has posted you at its opium factory in Bankipur for a reason, my dear fellow! You have a job to do. And let me tell you, it is not your job to feel sorry for poor Indian peasants and petition the Company on their behalf.'

'But, sir . . .' protested Jenkins, keeping pace with his senior as he walked busily around the factory. 'I want to ask if–'

'Look Jenkins,' Hopkins cut him short, 'I have far more important things to handle here. You do understand that the monopoly the Company has enjoyed all these years is to be withdrawn. We will be facing competition. There are targets to meet. The pressure is mounting every day. We have bigger problems.'

Jenkins hesitated and looked out the window. The sun was setting behind the ramparts of Fort William in Calcutta, the bastion of British power in India. To his right, he noticed boats bobbing up and down in the waters of the Hooghly. At the jetty, scrawny brown-skinned men hauled huge chests of opium on to barges which would take them further down the river, towards the ships. From there, they'd make their way to Canton and Shanghai. On the other side, there were hundreds of others huddled about at the pier, preparing to embark on long sea voyages that would take them to the opposite end of the world—to work on sugar plantations in British colonies in America. Jenkins sighed and wondered if those men would ever see their homes again.

'You ought not to be so sympathetic!' Hopkins' voice boomed from the back, almost as if he had read his mind. 'You understand how important it is for opium supplies to continue unabated, don't you?' asked Hopkins, looking towards the waterfront through the large glass windows. 'These are the wheels of the British empire. They simply have to be kept moving.'

Jenkins looked nervously at his shoes. Something about this whole sordid affair made him uncomfortable.

'It is not our job to question. It is our job to *obey!*' Hopkins offered his counsel, placing his hands on his junior's shoulders.

Jenkins nodded and gave half a smile. The sale of opium to China was shuttling more than £2 million a year into the lockers of the British East India Company. The tax from its sale funded the British Royal Navy, the foundation of its global empire. The supplies simply could not be halted.

'Besides, we shouldn't feel that sorry! After all, the Company is providing loans to farmers to cover the cost of rent and seed and fertilizer!' Hopkins continued, putting his hands in his pockets as the two gazed out towards the pier. 'C'mon! We also advance them money for digging wells and improving their land. Can't get better than that!'

Jenkins said nothing.

'And our loans are interest-free, unlike those offered by the village moneylenders. We're being generous!'

'Hmm . . .' Jenkins continued to listen.

'By this count, I would imagine the peasants who have been given licences to cultivate poppy by the British East India Company have a far better deal than the rest!' Hopkins laughed.

'That may be so, sir,' nodded Jenkins.

'Then, I am unable to understand what your problem is . . .'

'I am merely conveying their concerns to you, sir.'

'Well, their concerns are of no concern to *me*!' exclaimed Hopkins, walking over to greet a visitor who had just entered through the door.

'Ah! Mr Readymoney! You had a good one today!'

The visitor was a fair-skinned man dressed in a smart suit. 'Indeed!' he smiled, shaking Hopkins warmly by his hand.

'Meet our Asst. Sub Deputy posted at Bankipur,' said Hopkins, motioning Jenkins to come closer. 'This is the young man who makes sure you get your supplies up here on time!'

'And this my dear Jenkins, is Mr Readymoney, who shall I say, is one of the wealthiest merchants here in Calcutta. Much of the opium that you send us passes into the hands of Mr Readymoney, whose firm then ships it to China. They also happen to have bought the bulk from today's auction,' he said cheerfully.

'Pleased to meet you, Mr Jenkins,' said Mr Readymoney. As Jenkins shook hands with the visitor, his eyes widened in surprise. He couldn't believe that the man who stood before him was an Indian! All the Indians he had seen and met until then in Patna were poor, brown and obedient. But Mr Readymoney looked nothing like them!

What's more, his entire demeanour was different. Dressed in a crisp tailored suit with a bow tie to match, this wealthy Indian merchant of Calcutta looked much like an Englishman. The colour of his skin and his name even more so!

'I hear,' began Mr Readymoney, turning to Hopkins once again, 'that England has won the war in China!'

'Indeed!' said Hopkins, leading the way to his cabin and signalling the peon to get them some tea. 'I just received the good news myself,' he said, closing the door behind him and offering his guests a seat.

'And I hear,' said Mr Readymoney, sinking into a chair, 'that a treaty has been signed between the British and the Chinese at Nanjing to end the war. What exactly has been agreed upon?'

Jenkins drew up a chair beside the visitor, still staring clumsily at the fair-skinned Indian who spoke flawless English. *This was unreal.*

'Yes,' replied Hopkins. 'You heard right. The war has ended and as we had expected, the English have won. The Chinese have agreed upon some terms.'

'Does that mean . . .' Mr Readymoney asked softly, drawing himself closer to Hopkins as the peon entered, balancing a tray containing a tea cozy and fine Chinese porcelain cups and saucers in his hand.

'Does this mean that the sale of opium to China will be affected?' It was quite evident that the Indian was worried about his business, which was built around the sale of opium to China.

Hopkins turned to Mr Readymoney with an all-knowing look. 'The treaty of Nanjing makes no mention of opium!'

Mr Readymoney raised his eyebrows.

Jenkins gaped at him.

The Chinese emperor had bitterly opposed the sale of opium by the British in Chinese territory. *But naturally*, Jenkins thought, for his people were heavily addicted to the drug and lay wasted in opium dens across the country instead of engaging in work. Lin Tse-Hsu, his governor-general in Canton had destroyed hundreds of chests of opium by throwing them into the sea, triggering an all-out war. Thousands—both Chinese and British—had lost their lives in this war. People were calling it the Opium War.

And the treaty ending the Opium War made no mention of opium? What in heaven's name, thought Jenkins.

'The Chinese have allowed the English to operate from five of their ports. The island of Hong Kong stands leased to England for a 100 years! In addition, the Chinese shall pay England compensation! The costs for damages,' laughed Hopkins, proud of the achievements of the East India Company in China.

'Compensation for *their* damages?' Mr Readymoney shook his head, unable to believe what he was hearing. 'So . . . the treaty really makes no mention of opium?'

'None at all, my dear fellow,' replied Hopkins, pouring his visitors some tea.

'But the war . . . The Chinese emperor fought the war to stop opium from getting into China!' uttered Jenkins, unable to understand.

'Well, let's say that the emperor has been made to eat his own words!' Hopkins said, rubbing his palms gleefully.

'So, what you are saying in effect is that the supply of opium can continue without interruption?'

'Absolutely!' nodded Hopkins, picking up his cup of piping hot tea.

'This is absolutely incredible!' Jenkins whispered, sliding back into his chair.

'So, things can go on as they are then?' asked Mr Readymoney, seeking confirmation.

'Yes, indeed!' Hopkins got up and walked up to his window to watch chests of opium being loaded on barges. 'In fact, we must be shipping out all that opium . . . and *more* to China,' he added, raising a toast with the cup in his hands. 'So that we and our dear friends in England may continue to enjoy the best Chinese tea!'

3

SHANGHAI

Robert Fortune sat nervously stiff in his boat as he watched chests of opium floating past him on small barges, paddled by Chinese men carrying the smuggled goods further up into little towns in the countryside. It was all a clandestine affair, this.

'What business does your master have here?' he heard a curious onlooker making enquiries behind him.

Fortune's stomach tightened although he made it a point not to react. If anybody in these parts were to find out that he was a foreigner, he'd be a dead man. For he had no business being here. Like the chests of opium, his presence in China was illegal.

'My master is Sing Wa,' replied Wang, the assistant who Robert Fortune had so carefully chosen upon his arrival in China, '. . . is very big merchant from up north.'

'Hmmm . . .' the onlooker snorted looking at Fortune, clearly not convinced. Robert Fortune stood out in China like a sore thumb. Nearly a foot taller than every man around, his nose was too sharp and his cheeks too pink. His shoulders were too broad, gait too imposing and his eyes much too large. Clearly, he was no Chinese. The blue silk buttoned gown and padded coat along with long flowing trousers that Wang had insisted he put on, did remarkably little to give him the appearance of a local. Fortune had even shaved off his hair, save a little tuft that was braided into a plait. But even that could not mask his European features.

'Do you know what happened to Shizu, my cousin who tried to smuggle a Westerner in through the river?' asked the voice animatedly. Fortune could feel the intent gaze of the man boring into his back. 'Shizu and the foreigner were beaten and tortured! It is forbidden to take foreigners inside.' the onlooker continued, not believing the elaborate network of prestigious connections that Wang had spun to make Fortune appear like a credible businessman from the north of the country.

'My master . . . No Westerner he!' Wang pretended to laugh as he replied in Pidgin—a mix of Chinese, English, Portuguese and Hindi that was spoken in the Chinese port cities. 'My master is rich merchant of fine porcelain from beyond Great Wall. Now you bugger off and make haste! And load the luggage carefully! Or you'll have no food to take home to your children today!' Wang said loudly, assuming a sense of authority as he dispatched the man off with a barrage of instructions before he could open his mouth.

Fortune heaved a sigh of relief, glad to have Wang by his side. The assignment he had taken on was a risky affair. No Westerner had before him, entered the deep heart of China. No foreigner was permitted there.

But it was worth the risk: the best tea grew in the southern hills, deep inside China. The brew that had the English addicted. Thousands and thousands of chests of tea were making their way from China into England each year, for the English had grown used to gulping down copious amounts of tea. It had become a national addiction. And it was draining the English coffers. An alternative simply had to be found.

But tea was a prized secret of the Chinese empire. Just like silk had been. The Chinese were not going to let it out easily.

And so, Scottish botanist Robert Fortune found himself employed on a secret mission of the British East India Company. His job: to get into the heart of China and smuggle the secret tea leaf out. A job for which he had mastered Chinese, taken on a fake identity, disguised himself, bribed, cheated and put his life at risk. The enormity of the task weighed heavily on Fortune's shoulders.

As the boat pulled out of the quay, Fortune's mind was put to rest.

The fenced plots of little villages soon came into view. Fortune gazed at the neat patches of farmland growing wheat and rice, enjoyed the view of the tiny pagodas and temples nestled in the distant scraggy mountains, marvelled at the beauty of the waterfalls and bamboo groves. The Chinese countryside was full of the most beautiful roses and chrysanthemums, blooming jasmines and bleeding hearts. Flowers of every colour covered the hills. Oranges, melons and bountiful fruits of various kinds. A delight for a botanist. Fortune couldn't wait to get digging in those hills and take back with him whatever he could to England. He imagined his collection jars and boxes bursting with cuttings and saplings, seeds and samples.

And of course tea—the prized treasure.

If only he could pull this off, he thought to himself, it would go down in history as the greatest act of espionage the world had ever seen.

With that thought rolling over in his head, he sat back and eagerly awaited the destination—a quaint village in the Anhui Province.

4

HANGZHOU

When Wang and Fortune finally reached the village after a long and tiring journey, they received a warm reception.

'Welcome! We welcome you,' the old man, whom Wang introduced as the village elder, bowed before Fortune.

'Thank you!' said Fortune, bowing back, glad to be in the Chinese countryside, away from the port cities marked by the din of money, business and opium dens.

Fortune much preferred being amidst orchards of oranges and grapefruit, apricots and peaches, hemmed in by bushes of gardenia and roses of every hue. At the end of the day, he was a botanist. Not a spy.

'This is my uncle,' said Wang. 'You can live in this house during your stay here.'

'It is a pleasure to have you here,' said Wang's uncle softly in Chinese, inviting Fortune into the patio and pouring him a cup of freshly brewed green tea.

'This is wonderful,' exclaimed Fortune, inhaling the subtle aroma of the brew. 'You grow the best tea here!'

'We have been doing so for centuries!' the old man said with a smile, proud of the quality of his tea gardens.

'I am delighted to be here,' continued Fortune, unable to mask his interest in the subject any more. 'I would love to learn how you grow and brew the tea.'

The old man looked pleased. 'You have come to the right place, my son!' he said. 'These hills are the birthplace of tea!'

Fortune looked around the green hills. Nestled amidst the slopes of the Su La Mountains, the Anhui Province in east China had been the place that had brought him halfway around the world. Pirate attacks and ill-health, security checks and seasickness—he had braved them all to get here. It now seemed completely worth the while.

'Although it might seem like a simple affair,' the old man began, pointing to his little cup, 'brewing tea perfectly is a task that requires experience.'

Fortune listened attentively as the elderly man told him how the leaves were to be collected and dried and brewed to perfection, making a mental note of every detail which he would then diligently enter into his diary. None except the Chinese knew how tea was grown or processed. It was a secret they held dear. And now it was finally to be within Fortune's grasp.

'Tea can only grow on hill slopes,' the old man counselled him the next day as they set out for a walk in the hills. The poor man opened up his home and heart to the foreigner, not doubting for a second that the man was a spy. 'For it needs water but not too much. It needs sunlight, but not too much!' he smiled through the wrinkled skin on his face.

Fortune couldn't help wondering if the old man had any inkling that he was giving out state secrets to a foreigner. He put aside the thought.

'There is only one tea bush,' the man continued, answering Fortune's query. 'The white tea and the green tea and the black tea . . . they are not different at all!' he laughed. 'They all come from the same bush. It is only a matter of how they are processed.'

Fortune walked along, baffled by his discovery. It had for long been assumed that all the varieties of tea came from different species of plants. The truth made him smile. The source, the origin, was one! It was going to be easier than he thought!

Over the next few weeks, Fortune traversed the slopes of the Su La Mountains, along with his retinue of assistants and coolies, assembled by Wang from the villages nearby. Every little home on the hills had its own little patch of tea bushes at its rear. Fortune visited dozens of tea gardens and spoke at length to farmers and monks, extracting every little secret about growing, harvesting, producing and brewing the best tea.

His staff, diligently trained by him to take cuttings and crafts for the collection, marched behind him. Fortune had taught them to use blotting paper, to constantly keep a check for mould, remove insects that could harm the collection and how to use special Wardian cases, that he had brought along to transport plants back to England. They were a botany laboratory on the move!

The trusting villagers and naive old monks, curious about the stranger from the north, scurrying about the mountain slopes on a sedan chair with porters and coolies in tow and trunks of glass boxes and collection jars with seeds and saplings, were only too happy when he stopped by to talk to them. They shared open-heartedly all that they knew with him, not once doubting that he was here to steal their secrets and betray their trust.

Wang's family made the most gracious of hosts. Poor though they were, they took great care of their guest, as was the tradition in this part of the world. Fortune was surprised to note how cultured and refined a Chinese peasant could be. Even the poor were literate and read poetry! And without exception, they all had a daily bath. Unlike his countrymen back home!

As his mission neared completion, Fortune watched over his vast collection like a mother watching over a sleeping baby. Over 15,000 plant species! Carefully collected, sampled and catalogued to take back home. Fortune could have cried. It was an impossible feat. And he had pulled it off.

When it was time for Fortune to leave, farmers and monks of the region gathered to bid him goodbye. The village elder handed him a gift. 'This is a little talisman,' he said, placing a tiny wooden artefact in Fortune's palm, 'May it bring you good luck and take you safely home!'

Fortune felt a slight tug at his heartstrings. A short moment of remorse for cheating those who had offered him their home and hearth. He looked into the eyes of the people who had welcomed and trusted him and it pained him for just a moment.

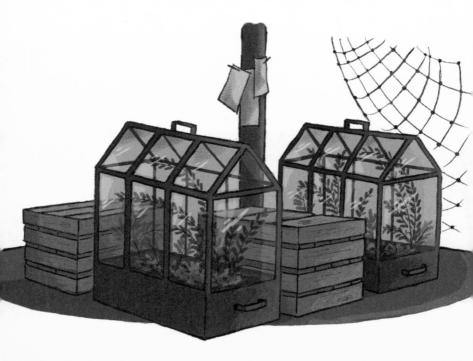

He thanked them quickly and turned away. After all that he had been through, he could not afford to stop. Remorse could not be allowed to get in his way.

As the coolies picked him up on the sedan chair to take him across the mountains to the port, Fortune said a quick prayer of gratitude. Luck had favoured him thus far. Could he get out alive?

5

DARJEELING

*S*o *this was Darjeeling*, Jenkins noted, taking in the cool mountain air into his lungs. The doctor had advised him to spend some time in the hills to recover from his illness. 'Time away from the hot and dusty plains would do you some good,' the doctor had said. A prescription he recommended for the better health and long life of any British officer stationed in India. Jenkins looked around.

The land had been surveyed and mapped. The forests cut and cleared. The timber carted off and sold.

Cottages for the planters. Barracks for the workers. Club for the officers.

Little roads zigzagged up the hills. A blanket of mist hung over rows upon rows of neatly planted bushes.

In every direction, as far as the eyes could see, there was tea, tea and more tea.

Jenkins had to admit he liked the place. The weather was incredible. The air, crisp and fresh. It rained, but not too much. The sun came out, but not too much. It seemed perfect to him.

And it was perfect for tea.

'Did Fortune bringing in all this tea from China?' he asked in surprise, turning to the supervisor of the tea gardens, with whom he had set out for a walk.

'All the tea bushes here are the babies of Fortune's find! Yes!' the supervisor nodded.

'I find it absolutely incredible!' Jenkins exclaimed, spinning around. Tea bushes sprouted in every direction, as far as his eyes could see. People huddled about, with baskets strapped to their shoulders, picking out the tea leaves. Still others collected them in piles and weighed them on scales. The day was about to wind down in the tea estate. In the distance, Jenkins noticed giant trees falling to the ground as more forest land was being cleared to make way for an extension of the tea gardens.

'And what about all this know-how?' Jenkins asked. 'Did Fortune also train all these people on picking and growing tea?'

'Believe it or not . . . he managed to smuggle a bunch of Chinese tea workers out of China!' the supervisor replied. 'But they are giving us a tough time now. They know we can't do without them,' he said, slightly miffed.

'So what's next then?'

'We are trying to get the local people trained to pick the right way. It is necessary,' the supervisor said, leading Jenkins towards a bush, 'that the top two leaves and the bud in the centre are picked in a neat crisp cut, like this,' he demonstrated. 'Else the tea won't taste right.'

'I could do that!' laughed Jenkins. 'Honestly, managing a tea estate seems to me a far better job than running an opium factory!'

'Don't speak so soon,' the supervisor warned, 'we have our share of troubles here.'

'Like what?' Jenkins prodded.

'I have a big problem on my hands now. The Chinese workers are not co-operating. The locals don't want to work. They are a contented lot, happy with whatever they have. It's hard to get them to work in these tea gardens.'

'So, what is it that you intend to do?'

'Indentured labour,' the supervisor whispered, pulling his coat over his shoulders.

'But slavery is banned!' exclaimed Jenkins, puzzled.

'Not slavery,' the supervisor shook his head, his tone terse and stern. 'Indentured labour.'

Jenkins paused, turning his gaze towards his feet as he always did in those awkward moments. He tried to gauge the meaning of the supervisor's words, unscrambling it in his head, imagining its true purport. He wondered if it were just another name. Old wine in a new bottle.

'I need to keep the tea gardens working,' said the supervisor matter-of-factly, with a shrug of his shoulders, discerning Jenkins' thoughts.

Jenkins sighed, remembering the words he had heard, many months ago from his superior in Calcutta. The wheels of the empire had to be kept moving. It was not their job to question. Only to obey.

'So . . . how's this tea doing back in England?' he asked, as they returned to the Planter's Club.

'Darjeeling tea is trading well. It fetches the Company more than Chinese tea!' the supervisor said, looking pleased. 'All the effort is bearing fruit!'

They sat down in a veranda overlooking the tea gardens. The setting sun painted the hills in yellow and orange. The view was spectacular. Jenkins was handed a cup of tea in fine white china.

He savoured its gentle aroma, delighted in its freshness. He took a sip, closed his eyes and enjoyed the moment. Surely, it was the finest tea in the world.

Meanwhile, somewhere near Patna, Kanjilal strained his eyes under the dull light of the single kerosene lamp in his house to read from a little sheet of paper he had just received. The letter was in English, a language he could neither understand nor read. But a few words had been scribbled alongside in a script he could follow. His heart sank.

His petition had been dismissed. He could not grow millets or vegetables on his fields. He'd have to sow poppy and send the harvest to the Company Factory at Bankipur for the manufacture of opium. He and his fellow petitioners had no choice in the matter.

Elsewhere, clouded around a curtain of smoke in an opium den in Shanghai, Wang and his coolie friends splurged the little fortune they had made off the funny-looking white man who had paid them handsomely for a handful of seeds and saplings. *How silly of him*, they laughed.

And in London, a few officers of the British East India Company met to take stock of the year gone by. Their revenues were unprecedented. Their profits were soaring.

For the very first time in history, a company ruled the world.

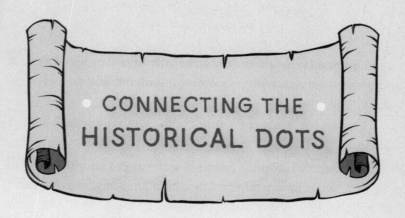

CONNECTING THE HISTORICAL DOTS

 FOOD

If you were to observe and make a note of everything you eat and drink, you would be surprised to find that many food items you consider to be a part of Indian cuisines were not a part of the Indian diet before!

Tea, regarded as a quintessentially Indian beverage, and coffee, also regarded as a traditional South Indian beverage, are not Indian in origin. While tea came to India from China (as narrated in the story), coffee is said to have originated in the region of Mocha in Yemen.

Some of the other ingredients that are today regarded as an intrinsic part of Indian cuisine also came to India during the colonial period—potatoes, chilies and tomatoes are some of the popular examples!

After the Industrial Revolution, the British made great advancements in science and technology. One of the areas in which it made great progress was botany. They realized the value of plants early on and a large part of the imperial project was spent in studying, sampling, understanding and even stealing plants.

The story of Robert Fortune and his theft of tea from China is true.

A Scottish botanist, Fortune was roped in by the British East India Company to travel to China and 'steal' tea. England had grown thirsty for this marvellous beverage from the East and was, in fact, spending a large amount of money in silver to pay for it. In order to even out their outflow, the British created a demand for opium in China by smuggling the drug into the country, despite it being banned by the Chinese emperor. Millions of Chinese became drug addicts and two wars, known as the 'Opium Wars' were fought between China and England as a result.

Due to their superior naval technology, Britain won both the wars and China had to cede or give up the territory of Hong Kong as payment for damages apart from a huge amount of money in fines. Here, India indirectly became a part of this ugly game as farmers in the country were forced to grow poppy and produce opium in order to ship to China. The rise of Bombay (now Mumbai) as a port and the wealth of many of its Parsi merchants had much to do with the opium exports to China.

Tea and opium were not the only plants that played a defining part in history.

As you have perhaps read, pepper and spices lured the Europeans to find a sea route to India, changing the course of world history. Find out more about the origin and history of other plants and food items on your plate. Not only will you discover their fascinating past but also learn a new and fun way of looking at history!

UNBOX THE PAST: FIND HISTORY HIDDEN IN THIS STORY.

 ## THE MAD HATTER'S TEA PARTY

Tea first made it to England in the 1660s. It was a part of the dowry paid by the Portuguese Princess Catherine of Braganza when she married Charles II of England. Along with a chest of tea (as the Portuguese princess was very fond of tea!), many islands of Bombay were given as a part of the dowry! Slowly, tea-mania gripped the entire country and all of England was drinking cups and cups of tea, triggering off the culture of tea parties and high tea.

 ## TURNING OPIUM INTO TEA

Once the British had a taste of tea, they absolutely loved it. At the time, all the tea of the world came from China, where it was grown and consumed. The Chinese, however, did not want any of the British goods in return. They wanted the British to pay for the tea with silver, the currency used in China.

But the British wished to have the silver and drink their tea too!

The export of tea from China to England was mounting by the day because the English were hooked. The British East India Company looked for an easier way of getting tea into England, so they came up with two incredible plans.

1. Stealing the tea bush out of China;
2. Reversing the tea trade with the help of opium.

Opium, a drug made from poppy seeds, had been used for many years as a painkiller across the world. The British East India Company noticed the demand for opium in China and the high-quality opium grown in central India and devised a unique plan.

They began shipping out huge quantities of opium from India into China illegally, as the sale of opium in China was illegal. With this, the Chinese silver began flowing into their coffers.

The Chinese silver that the British earned in exchange for the opium, funded a large part of the operations of the Company.

In 1834, the Governor-General Lord William Bentinck had set up a Tea Committee to investigate and make recommendations about the most suitable areas to grow tea in India. With the theft of tea from China, followed by its successful introduction in India, the demand for tea in England began to be met from the tea gardens of Darjeeling and other hilly regions in India.

It was a win-win situation for the British. They had the silver and could drink their tea too!

 OPIUM AND THE RISE OF BOMBAY

Opium had been used as a painkiller for several centuries. However, its production had always been kept under control. When the British East India Company arrived on the scene, they obtained a monopoly for the opium produced in India. The Company did not, however, sell it directly to the customers. The opium was auctioned to traders who in turn, smuggled it into China.

In the 1790s, about 4000 chests of opium were sold by auction in Calcutta. In less than a century, 15,000 chests of opium were being auctioned in Calcutta to be smuggled into China. This rise in opium trade was fuelled by the British.

The wealth and prominence of the city of Mumbai (then Bombay) was founded largely upon the roaring opium trade that took place from there. Parsi merchants were the leading opium dealers of the time. Many Parsis, including the illustrious Jamshedji Tata and Jamsetjee Jeejeebhoy, made their fortunes from the opium business.

 BOTANICAL GARDEN

The Botanical Garden of Calcutta (previously known as the Royal Botanical Garden and currently the Acharya Jagdish Chandra Bose Indian Botanic Garden) was set up in 1786 for identifying plants that had commercial value. Far from being a pleasure paradise, the garden was the centre of critically significant activities of the British East India Company.

It was a place where economically useful plants such as teak, tobacco, coffee, indigo, etc., came to Calcutta from India and elsewhere, for distribution to different parts of the empire.

The Gardens were responsible for the introduction of nutmeg, cinnamon, cloves, peppers and other food items to India. Quinine, used in anti-malaria medicines, comes from the bark of a tree found in South America, and was brought here to be introduced within India to help British officers who were plagued with malaria. Tea was introduced in the Himalayan mountains after it was brought to the Gardens from China.

The Great Banyan, believed to be over 250 years old, was one of the main attractions of the Botanical Gardens, until it was destroyed during a cyclone in 2020.

 ## THE NEW SLAVERY

After slavery was abolished in British colonies in the early 19th century, they had to resort to other methods to find labourers for their plantations. The system of slavery was replaced by the 'indentured labour system', which differed little from slavery in practice. Under the indentured system, labourers were bound to a plantation through a contract and anybody who violated the contract by leaving, was given harsh punishments by the planters, who acted as a legal authority.

Under this system, labourers lived a harsh life with meagre wages, little food and a high risk of disease and epidemics. Labourers were also treated very badly, put under lock and key, flogged and so on. 'Indentured labour' was often referred to as the new form of slavery.

 ## DARJEELING AND TEA

Darjeeling is situated in the foothills of the Himalayas and is located in the state of West Bengal. Most of the tea that one sees in Darjeeling today, owes its origin to the tea seeds and saplings that were smuggled in by Robert Fortune from China.

While Darjeeling is world-famous for its tea gardens today, two centuries ago, it was no more than a little hamlet in the remote hills, surrounded by dense tropical and subtropical forests inhabited by Tibeto-Burmese people. As the cold, damp climate and constant mist of Darjeeling were ideal for the production of tea, the British East India Company decided to experiment by growing Chinese tea here.

The experiment was a roaring success. Tea from India, particularly Darjeeling, replaced Chinese tea in the British market. Even today, Darjeeling is considered a premium and exclusive brand of tea. So much so, that the *Darjeeling* tag began to be used by manufacturers in order to pass off various varieties of tea as the superior tea of Darjeeling. The Tea Board of India had to step in and Darjeeling has now been recognized as a geographical indicator, meaning that only tea from Darjeeling can claim that label. Do you know some other Indian products that have been protected as geographical indicators? Find out more.

 MAN-MADE FAMINE

Several famines have hit India over the years, but it is said that their number and intensity increased in the late 18th and 19th century due to the policies of the British. The great Bengal famine that took place in the late 1860s was one of the worst in Indian history. There was widespread starvation and the death toll was estimated at over 10 million! That is about the entire population of Portugal today!

Apart from poor harvest and a failed monsoon, the British East India Company's policies were largely to blame. They increased land taxes which discouraged production and they encouraged the replacement of food crops with cash crops such as poppy (opium) and indigo—leading to reduced food availability.

The farmers being compelled to grow poppy in this story captures this situation.

STORIES OF
POWER
AND
PERSPECTIVE

THE MERCHANT
OF SURAT

1

HAR HAR MAHADEV!

'RUN!! Run for your life!' two men behind Haridas pushed him out of their way as they scurried through the narrow lanes in the darkness.

Haridas' throat went dry. A chilling fear gripped him. The thundering sound of approaching horses filled the nervous night air. Light from fires raging all around the ransacked city lit up the sky. A blanket of smoke enveloped everything as flames licked at wood and thatch. At a distance, the sound of war cries mixed with wailing moans.

Haridas hurried home and closed the door behind him.

'Baba! Thank God you're safe!' Lakshmi bolted to her father.

'Yes, yes . . . Baba is back. Don't worry,' Haridas swooped his little girl in his arms, wiping away tears on her horror-stricken face.

Suddenly, a bloodcurdling scream rang out from the distance.

'Har Har Mahadev!' the thundering war cry of Shivaji's soldiers galloping through the streets shook the walls of their little home.

Grabbing hold of his daughter's hand, Haridas dashed to the little room at the back of the house. Cowering under the charpoy of the dimly lit room, he closed his eyes to pray.

'Baba, why is Shivaji Maharaj attacking Surat?' sobbed little Lakshmi, trembling beside him. 'Why is he doing this?'

Haridas looked into his daughter's wide eyes. The innocence took him back in time. To a day thirty long years ago. Back when a similar question had puzzled him. When death had come knocking at his door.

2

SCOURGE

Little Haridas looked up and saw the great famine sweep over Surat like a cloud of locusts descending upon a field. The monsoons had failed for the third year in a row. The fields of bajra and other millet were lifeless and barren—brown and dust-coloured. There was nothing to eat. *Nothing*. Those who had any strength left in their bodies had fled the village in the hope of finding food elsewhere. Those that couldn't move, watched and waited for death to consume them.

'We *must* leave the village,' Haridas' father cried. Only a few days back, his mother and two brothers had perished. 'Perhaps we will find some hope elsewhere . . . we must . . .'

And so they had made their way. Sitting atop his father's shoulders, walking through villages under the scorching sun, Haridas saw the dead piled up on the streets and along the ditches. They trudged along with no food or shelter for days. Wherever they went, the story was the same. The rains had failed. The crops had been destroyed. No food. Thousands dead. Despair and hopelessness all around.

Wandering for days with little to eat or drink, father and son approached the gates of Surat. *Surely, the city that was so fabulously wealthy would bring them some relief,* thought Haridas' father, as he joined the crowds thronging its gates.

'Make way! Make way!' a guard mounted atop a brown steed was clearing the streets behind them. 'The *badshah* approaches! Make way!'

Badshah Shah Jehan! Haridas' spirits soared.

'The king is coming! Baba, Badshah Shah Jehan is coming!' he repeated to his father in excitement.

Back in his village, he had heard many tales about kings and queens from his grandmother. From travellers, he'd been astonished to learn about the splendid Mughal Court in Agra. About the gleaming Peacock Throne and the dazzling Koh-i-noor diamond. But he had never imagined he'd see the Mughal Emperor Shah Jehan with his own eyes some day!

'Allah! Thank you for answering our prayers!' cried an old and crippled woman hobbling along behind them, looking heavenward.

'Not too long ago, Badshah Shah Jehan was the governor of Surat,' another said, raising everyone's hope. 'He will surely help us.'

Haridas craned his neck to catch a glimpse of the royal elephant. *How fortunate he was to run into the king at such a moment in his life!*

Finally, a great column of dust appeared on the horizon. Horses and elephants emerged from the distance, followed by row upon row of infantry.

'What an army!' Haridas exclaimed, climbing up on his father's shoulders to gaze at the unending sea of soldiers and animals.

Hundreds of fine Arabian horses marched along, forming a sizeable cavalry. There were thousands of elephants carrying all sorts of things from tents to bathtubs. Cartloads of utensils and weapons. Cannons and muskets. The entire palace appeared to be moving with the badshah. Soldiers and guards. Doctors and priests. Cooks and entertainers. Porters and washermen. Droves of cattle for slaughtering. Cartloads of fodder for the animals. *Were they really in the midst of a famine?* Haridas rubbed his sleepy eyes.

When the emperor's elephant finally came into view, it was nearing dusk. 'Badshah Shah Jehan!' Haridas screamed, pointing to the royal elephant.

Desperate pleas and wailing began as the Emperor approached. 'Help us! Help us, Badshah! Take pity on us! We are dying!'

The emperor peeped out from behind the curtain of his howdah. *He'll stop now and help us,* Haridas said to himself. *All that food the army carries will be distributed to the hungry.* Haridas waited, like all the others around him standing by the side of the road, with folded hands and hopeful eyes.

The badshah drew the curtain. His elephant marched on. His large army followed. Past parched lands. Past the dying millions. Past Haridas and his father.

As an afterthought, the emperor ordered to have some soup kitchens opened for his suffering subjects before continuing onward. And then he was off to wage war upon the Deccan to enlarge his empire in the middle of a famine.

'How can Badshah Shah Jehan fight a war when his people are dying, Baba?' Haridas asked his father. 'Why is he doing this?'

His father stared blankly into his eyes.

3

A NEW BEGINNING

'Har Har Mahadev!' the war-cry arose once again. Galloping horses thudded past outside the mud walls, drawing Haridas out of the past. He drew Lakshmi closer. Her eyes, gleaming in the moonlight streaming in through the window, were still looking into his—waiting for an answer.

'Let me tell you a story.' Haridas whispered, wrapping his arms around his daughter, without taking a moment to think it through. It was the only distraction he could provide.

'After the famine had forced us to leave our village and home,' Haridas began, joining the thread of thoughts in his mind, 'Dadaji and I . . . we wandered about hopelessly for several days.' Lakshmi stopped sobbing and forgot momentarily the thudding of horses from the street outside. 'I was just as old as you are now,' Haridas recounted, placing his hand upon her head. 'And just as scared,' he added with a sigh.

'What happened then, Baba?' Lakshmi asked, drying her eyes.

'Surat!' answered Haridas with a slight smile. 'Surat happened to us. Surat turned our lives around. And we survived!' he said.

'Dadaji found work at the ship-building site in the city . . . The waters of the Tapti that flow through this city renewed our hopes and sustained us. He pleaded with the seth there. A number of workers at the yard had left after the famine, so Dadaji was fortunate to find some work there.'

'What did *you* do, Baba?'

'Me? I helped Dadaji, I did what I could. There is plenty to do at a ship-building yard. Have you seen a big ship?'

Lakshmi nodded.

'Large amounts of wood are used to first make the hull of the ship. Then the planking is placed inside it. The planks and the hull are sewn together with hemp. Then the masts have to be erected, the sail cloth stitched and rigged on the masts with strong ropes, the blank spaces between the planks have to be filled to make the ship waterproof. There is much work at a ship-building site.'

Lakshmi began to forget about the mayhem outside.

'One day,' continued Haridas, 'I saw a rich man talking to the seth at the docks. He wore a fine silk waistcoat and a large white turban. He was the wealthiest looking person I had ever seen. Imagine my surprise when I learnt that this man had come to the seth's office to place an order for ten ships!' said Haridas, spreading out his ten fingers before Lakshmi's little face.

'I learnt later that his name was Virji Vora sahib. He was the richest merchant in Surat. And perhaps the richest in the country. Even the firangis borrowed money from him!'

'Really? The English sahibs borrowed money from him?'

'Yes! Not just the English but the others too. The Portuguese, the Dutch and the French. They all came to Vora sahib to ask for his help.'

'What happened then?'

'Your Baba did the same thing!' Haridas chuckled. 'I told Dadaji that I too would go to Virji Vora sahib and ask him for some money to trade. Dadaji wasn't impressed with the idea. But I told him I didn't want to be sewing planks on ships all my life!'

'And did Vora sahib help you?'

Haridas smiled and shook his head. '"Can you put the cart ahead of the donkey?" was what Vora sahib asked my father.'

Lakshmi covered her mouth and giggled.

'You want to trade but you know nothing about it!' he said to me. I stood there looking at the ground, deeply disappointed.

'"But I like your courage!" he said to me as I was about to leave. My eyes lit up and I turned back.'

'A ship with my goods leaves for Aden tomorrow. Will you go?' he asked.

'Dadaji was shaking his head. He had worked in the ship-building yard for over ten years but never thought about sailing out into the high seas. He had heard several dreadful tales of frightful storms and shipwrecks. But to my ears, it was sweet music. Many of the friends I had made in Surat were from trading families. Cloth, gems, precious stones, spices—they traded and made a lot of money. "Yes!" I said without a second thought or even consulting my father.'

'"Don't be silly!" Dadaji warned me. "The seas are festering with pirates! The Sanganian pirates, firangi pirates . . . there are plenty of them . . . Don't you know how dangerous it is?"'

'But I wouldn't hear any of it. Assuring Dadaji that I'd be all right, I decided to take Vora sahib up on his offer,' said Haridas, and paused to reflect about those bygone days.

'The next noonday sun found me on the deck of a massive ship, watching the endless blue ocean that lay at the mouth of the Tapti, in complete awe. That evening, I saw for the very first time, the orange sun set into the seas. The waves looked like they were on fire. It was the most spectacular sight my eyes had ever witnessed!'

Lakshmi waited to hear more.

'And just like the famine had done, that one event turned my life around.'

4

PEPPER NATION

'What happened then, Baba? Did you run into pirates?' asked Lakshmi, drawn in by her father's story. The sound of the horses had receded into the background. Lakshmi had stopped trembling.

'Many times!' Haridas chuckled. 'The firangi pirates with their guns are the deadliest of the lot!'

Lakshmi's eyes grew wide. Her father, even huddled as he was under the charpoy, appeared heroic to her.

'But why?' Lakshmi asked her favourite question. 'Why do these firangis come to India? Isn't it really far away from their home?'

Haridas nodded. 'Tremendously far,' he replied. 'It takes them over four months to come here from their country. The journeys are quite difficult and involve a lot of hardship. Without fresh food or water, many of them fall sick during the journey . . . some even die.'

'So why do they come here?' Lakshmi asked again. 'What for?'

'For pepper!'

'*Hain*? Pepper?' Lakshmi cocked her neck, her eyes narrowing in bewilderment.

Haridas smiled. Of course, it seemed unbelievable.

'Yes . . . pepper!' he said. 'And for our cotton. They say it's the best in the world,' he added proudly.

'So the firangis don't get pepper and cotton in their country?'

'No . . . they call our pepper "black gold". They value it as much as gold! And nobody can spin muslin cloth like our weavers can. The cloth they make in their countries is coarse.'

Lakshmi giggled. It seemed funny to her. The little *kaali miri*, or black pepper, that her mother pounded in the pestle almost daily to add flavour and aroma to the dal she cooked, had lured these strange white men halfway across the world. *How curious!*

'What about these men on horses, Baba? Are they here for pepper and cotton too?' asked Lakshmi.

'Well . . . Pepper and cotton have made Surat rich, beta,' sighed Haridas. 'Shivaji has come for the riches of Surat.' he added, reflecting upon his journey out of penury—weeks together at sea, months away from home, years upon years of hard work, overcoming storms and escaping pirates. Battling all odds, a famine-stricken young boy had emerged out of the dead weight of destiny to claim a decent life for himself.

Was everything he had achieved going to be taken away?

5

PLUNDER!

'This is Virji Vora's godown. Attack it!' a loud voice thundered from beyond the walls.

'This one godown alone will provide us with enough to sustain our army for months!' remarked another.

The cracking of a whip sliced through the cold night, followed by the thundering sound of a dozen hooves as they galloped towards the godown gates.

Haridas closed his eyes and prayed. The godown had goods worth several lakhs. The life of many ordinary people like him lay enmeshed within its walls—the labour of the spice growers in Kerala and the cotton farmers in Gujarat, the skill of the weavers of Kutch and the dyers upcountry. Together, the goods in the godown represented the toil and labour of thousands like him.

He heard the hordes break down the gates. He heard more horses approaching. He heard his heart pounding within his chest. Lakshmi clung to her father's arms, hiding her face in his sleeve to muffle her sobs.

'Ah ha! So this is it,' roared the commander, his voice laced with contentment. 'The wealth of Surat's richest man is all here. Soldiers! Ransack the godown!'

'Let the Mughal cowards hide behind the doors of their fortress and watch while their city burns!' a soldier laughed.

The Mughal administration that controlled Surat had left the people to defend themselves. The subedar had hidden himself in the fort, not caring to put up a fight against Shivaji. How ironic it was, thought Haridas. The might of the Mughals had come to naught before the Maratha warrior.

Peering helplessly from a corner of his window, Haridas watched as the soldiers looted the godown. Cartloads of spices. Bales of cotton. Piles of coarse cloth. Packs of fine muslin. Drums of dye. Boxes of opium. Goods worth lakhs—they ransacked it all. They seized everything of value and destroyed whatever they didn't find useful. Haridas watched the plunder, feeling utterly helpless.

'Onward to Vora's home!' the General astride the horse commanded. 'He must have plenty of gold and silver stashed inside his home!'

Vora sahib was by then an old man. As the horses galloped away, Haridas prayed for his master. For the man who had given him a second life.

After staying motionless for a long time, Haridas dared to move. 'You stay here,' he whispered to his daughter. 'I'll go out and check.'

'Please don't go, Baba!' cried Lakshmi. 'I'm scared.'

'They won't come back here now,' Haridas assured his daughter, as he opened the door. 'They've taken what they want. I will be back soon. You stay here.'

Haridas crept silently towards the godown. The spectacle made him sick. His head began to spin. 'Hey Ram!' he gasped.

In searching for the gold and silver, gems and pearls, the Maratha soldiers had ransacked everything. Cloves and cinnamon lay strewn about as sacks of spices had been slashed through with swords. Bundles of coarse cloth and piles of sail cloth had been thrown around. Little puffs of cotton were flying out of the packages that had been kept ready for sailing. Jars of colourful dyes lay toppled on the ground, soiling the floor. Everything was destroyed.

Climbing atop the warehouse, Haridas looked out at the city that had made him. Fires raged in every corner and the cold January night air was filled with cries of anguish. The historic city of Surat, where merchants from all over the world came to realize their dreams, had been ravaged.

Haridas fell to his knees. Holding his head in his hands, he sobbed like a child.

For years, stories would be told about great kings, their dazzling palaces, their ruby-encrusted thrones and fine jewels. Bards would sing legends about warriors, recounting tales of their bravado, their valour, their greatness. Generations to come would know their names.

But would time stop to take note of the people? Of those like him whose lives had been crushed under the weight of the power games of kings and warriors? Would history remember ordinary people? Would they even count?

Or would they, Haridas mused, like the little peppercorn strewn about the courtyard—the peppercorn that had silently changed the world—be ground to dust?

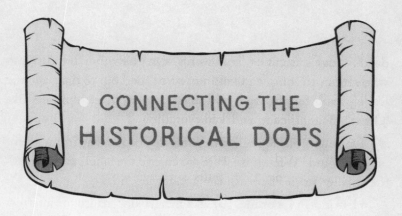

CONNECTING THE HISTORICAL DOTS

 VICTORY AND POWER

When World War II broke out in Europe, British Prime Minister Winston Churchill diverted food from India to provide buffer stock for Allied soldiers in the event of an invasion in Greece and Yugoslavia. In Bengal, the crop situation was made worse by a devastating cyclone that hit the region in 1942. Millions of Indians starved to death as a result of what came to be known as the Bengal Famine. Nearly 2000 people were dying each month in Calcutta.

When Churchill was notified about the conditions in India, he is believed to have said 'Well it's all their fault anyway for breeding like rabbits!'

Today, Churchill is hailed as a great war hero for defeating Hitler and the rise of fascist powers in World War II.

When you learn about famines in history books, the collective suffering and experiences of ordinary people are reduced to numbers with phrases like 'great famine', 'millions dead', 'huge casualties' and so on. On the other hand, kings who set out to conquer, explorers who sailed out to discover and leaders who fought wars to keep peace are given epithets like 'Great', 'Magnificent' and 'Honourable'.

Do you think labels like these create deep lasting impressions on your mind? What if we were to remove the labels and unearth the smaller stories beneath the greater legends?

Historically, famine has been a major cause of distress in India, leading to mass migration. The Deccan Famine of the 1630s described in this story was one of the many brutal famines to take place in India. Parents were recorded selling and giving away their children to anyone who could feed them. There are also some gruesome references of people consuming their own children.

While Shah Jehan had soup kitchens opened and disbursed money to the poor, he continued to wage war in the Deccan during this time. The money he spent on welfare was supposedly a paltry proportion of his immense wealth. During war, food grains were often diverted for use by the army, causing severe food shortages.

While Shivaji is said to have been sensitive regarding food stocks—even directing officials not to crush farmers for military needs—he looted Surat twice for its fabulous wealth in order to acquire resources for his fight against the Mughals.

You have no doubt heard about the fabulous wealth of the Mughals—from the Peacock Throne to the Kohinoor. Or about the brave conquests of the Guptas and Marathas. Or the constant battles between the Pallavas and Chalukyas. Of unending sagas of kings and dynasties, their battles and wars—with little mention of the price of all that glitz and glamour. Ordinary people like Haridas are somehow lost in those tales of power and valour.

Do you think history acquires more relevance and meaning when seen from the perspective of ordinary everyday objects and events?

UNBOX THE PAST: DISCOVER HISTORY HIDDEN IN THIS STORY.

 ## GUJARAT: THE HUB OF TRADE

Stretching for over 1600 miles, Gujarat has the longest coastline amongst all Indian states. This geographic feature allowed for the flourishing of many harbours and port cities. Bharuch, Khambat, Surat and Mandvi thrived as bustling centres of trade through centuries. Even today, ports like Alang, Bhavnagar, Kandla, Porbandar, etc., dot the coastline of Gujarat. Lothal, the oldest dry dock of the world, is also situated in Gujarat.

 ## THE STORY OF SURAT

The city of Surat, situated on the banks of the River Tapti was one of the largest trading centres of India in the 17th century. Drawn by its wealth and geographic position, early European colonizers established their factories in Surat, which was also a leading centre of banking and a source of capital. As the place of embarkation for the annual pilgrimage to Mecca, Surat held a special position. From amongst all the ports of the Indian Ocean in the 17th century, Surat enjoyed the largest volume of trade. Surat rose to prominence with the decline of Cambay or Khambat, which previously held prime position as a western port. Surat itself declined following the rise of Bombay.

FAMILY HISTORY HIDDEN IN NAMES

Several people from Gujarat own shops or businesses. If one were to delve deeper, one will find that behind this enterprising nature of a Gujarati, lie centuries of history. And behind that history lies the silent hand of geography. Given Gujarat's lengthy coastline, trade and commerce were the primary source of livelihood there. Surnames sometimes hold clues to the nature of the family trade. Here are some examples.

Kapadia	Cloth merchant (kapad/kapda = cloth)
Seth	Trader/Head
Kothari	Storehouse owner/caretaker (manager of the *kotha*)
Bhandari	Storehouse keeper (keeper of the *bhandar*)
Gandhi	Perfume seller/grocer (derived from *gandh* meaning fragrance)
Shroff/Sharaf	Banker/money-changer/cashier
Dalal	Agent/Broker
Munim	One in charge of money

 SHIVAJI AND HIS RAID OF SURAT

Having continuously battled Mughal forces in the Deccan, Shivaji was in dire need of resources. Surat was the main port of the Mughal Empire. Shivaji looted Surat in January 1664. Fearing for his life, the Mughal chief who was in charge of the city hid himself in the fort. Shivaji's soldiers are said to have attacked the warehouses of wealthy Indian merchants, save that of a merchant named Parekh, who was known to be a very charitable man. It is said that the raiders obtained barrels of gold, money, pearls, gems and precious wares—estimated to be worth 50,000 pounds from Virji Vora, who is said to have been one of the richest persons of that time.

Shivaji raided Surat once again in 1670.

 ## PEPPER CHANGED WORLD HISTORY

The story of India's colonization begins with the lure of pepper. The Portuguese were in search of pepper when they first arrived in India. They were followed by the Dutch, the French and then the English. If it weren't for pepper, the history of colonialism may have been very different. It won't be wrong to say therefore that pepper changed the course of world history.

 ## THE CRAFTS OF KUTCH

Kutch has been known for its master craftsmanship for centuries. You may have heard about Bandhani, the tie and dye textile work and the beautiful mirror-work called Abhla. Kutch has also been known for weaving, block printing, various styles of embroidery and several other crafts. Surat, along with the ports of Kutch, were the doorways through which this fine craftsmanship of Kutch reached the world.

THE SAILOR OF KOZHIKODE

1

THAT SINKING FEELING

'Sail Ho!' yelled Yusuf, waving down the flag with his right hand, even as he continued to peer into the looking glass.

Suleiman, the grey-haired helmsman looked out into the clear waters. It had been a long journey for all aboard the Miri. He couldn't wait to return home. The hundreds on board, returning from the holy pilgrimage to Mecca, were just as restless to get back. 'What's the matter?' he shouted back at Yusuf, who was perched up on the crow's nest.

'We need to slow down!' Yusuf screamed back, so he could be heard above the roar of the wind.

'Whatever for?' the Nakhuda sahib shot back. The captain was as eager as everyone else to get back home and could see nothing but clear blue waters before him.

'I see some ships. There!' Yusuf pointed out. 'Christian ships!'

'Allah! Portuguese?' asked the Nakhuda sahib, his interest piqued.

Yusuf nodded.

'Let me see!' said the Nakhuda, climbing up the rope ladder to join Yusuf at the lookout point. Sure enough, there were

Portuguese ships—with large red Christian crosses emblazoned on their white sails. Not one but dozens of them. It was a blockade!

Ships had been plying in and out of the Indian waters into Arabia, Africa and the Far East for centuries, carrying spices and silks, cotton and muslin, grains and precious stones. Kings and rulers had come and gone but none had tried to extend their control over the free waters. Trade had thrived without fear . . . till now.

But the coming of the Portuguese five years ago, under the command of a man named Vasco da Gama, had changed everything. The once peaceful waters had turned into a bloody battleground. Nobody was allowed to ply their ships in the Indian Ocean without a Portuguese *cartaz*. The ships that dared to operate without Portuguese permission were hounded and taught a lesson.

'Cut the sails! Slow down! Change tack!' the captain shouted, an uneasy feeling coming over him. *Pirates could be dealt with. They wanted wealth and they wanted to loot. The Portuguese were another game altogether,* he thought to himself. It was unclear what exactly they wanted. It filled him with a sense of foreboding.

'One can fight an enemy whose intentions are clear. It's hard to fight an enemy whose motives are unknown.' the Nakhuda sahib often told his crew.

'Keep good watch,' he ordered, putting a firm hand on Yusuf's young shoulders before vanishing below deck. 'I'll be right back!'

2

SITTING DUCK

Yusuf returned to his looking glass. One of the Christian ships was turning to make way towards them. The port holes on its side came into view. 'Allah!' Yusuf's pulse began to race. 'Over half a dozen cannons!' Yusuf wiped his sweaty palms on his trousers. He could hear his heart pounding.

'Hey!' Yusuf yelled to the helmsman below. 'They're coming for us!'

On the deck, all on board were going about their affairs like it were an ordinary day. Women sat around with their babies. Little children ran around on the sunny deck. Sailors attended to their tasks quietly while others played *aatu puli*, a game of cowrie shells, with some chalk and marbles under the raised forecastle of the ship. The sound of clanging pots and pans could be heard from below deck, where the ship's cook was preparing the day's meal.

In a corner, Yusuf's old parents were dozing away, tired after a long journey. Their life's longing to go to Mecca and complete the Hajj had finally come true. His wife Mariam sat by their side, cooing away into the ears of Kunju Ahmed, their two-year-old boy. They were expecting their second baby. Life was looking good.

Three ships with the large red crosses were getting closer. He could see figures of little people climbing up to the rigging and manoeuvring the sails. The ships were being made to turn to starboard. And he could see why. The cannons were now pointing straight at the Miri!

Allah! Where was the blessed captain!

Yusuf looked around desperately. They were in the open seas. No bay, no inlet, no channel anywhere in sight to back into and lay low. Moreover, the wind was favouring the Portuguese ships that were heading in their direction. *There's no escape*, he shuddered.

Yusuf decided to make a dash below deck to search for the captain. There was no time for discussion. They needed the captain's orders!

Just as he climbed down the rope ladder, the captain emerged with a party of men including the ship's master Jauhar al-Faqih, one of the wealthiest merchants of Kozhikode (Calicut) and the agent of the Sultan of Egypt. Clad in a purple silk gown and a string of pearls around his neck, al-Faqih seemed stoic and calm.

'What's going on?' he demanded, holding his palm over his eyes to shield them from the sun.

'Portuguese ships, sir!' Yusuf said, panting hard. 'They're coming for us. They have heavy cannons!'

Al-Faqih squinted his eyes against the glare to take a look.

'They're all around us!' Yusuf swallowed hard, as al-Faqih and the captain spun about to see three large caravels hovering around them like deathly clouds of doom.

The Miri, with all its 300 passengers, was trapped.

3

ADMIRAL OF INDIA

'What is it you want?' Jauhar al-Faqih demanded, not the least bit intimidated by the man who called himself the Admiral of India. A scraggy-looking Portuguese sailor quickly translated the words for his strange-looking captain who was dressed in a purple velvet shirt and odd-looking boots.

Vasco da Gama was miffed with the tone of al-Faqih's voice. He expected the Indians to be cowering in fear.

'Do you think I am a pirate?' he asked Jauhar al-Faqih in a threatening tone, stepping closer and staring into his eyes.

Al-Faqih stared back at da Gama without flinching. 'I carry some gold on my ship! Take it and let us go!'

'Damn you!' Da Gama spat on the ground 'So, you people *do* think I am a pirate!'

And then the admiral began to laugh. At first, he laughed menacingly, with an evil glint in his eyes. And then he held his stomach and laughed loudly, pointing repeatedly at al-Faqih and muttering something in Portuguese.

Yusuf stood behind his master and stared at the Portuguese captain, wondering if something was seriously wrong with the man. He was reminded of the poor tailor in his village who suffered from dementia.

'Some gold? You offer me *some* gold?' the translator managed to get some words across to them, through the incessant laughter of the Admiral.

'Your ships are in bad condition!' al-Faqih added. 'I can get your masts repaired!'

Da Gama's laughter escalated to a fever pitch. Yusuf began to feel worried.

'*You* will repair my ships? You?' Da Gama finally stopped laughing and turned to his men. 'Do you hear? This man offers to repair my ships!' he said aloud for all his crew to hear.

Yusuf swallowed hard. It seemed his master was getting off on the wrong foot. He recollected only too well, that horrific night, only a few months ago, when another Portuguese captain named Cabral had brought another fleet of Portuguese ships into Malabar. Cabral had bombarded Kozhikode with his guns and cannons because nobody had sold him spices to take back to Portugal!

For centuries, traders from China and Indonesia in the Far East to Arabia and Africa, even Rome in the West had come to India for spices. For the pepper and cloves of India were the best in the world. But they had all behaved like traders and bought the spices at the market price. These white men from some godforsaken place called 'Purtugal' had come for the spices too. But they wanted to buy them not by paying the market price but by the barrel of the gun! Yusuf whispered something into his master's ears.

'Ah! Is it spices that you want?' al-Faqih asked again. 'Don't I know that you Purtugalis have come halfway around the world in search of our spices?'

Da Gama turned to face al-Faqih. Yusuf noticed an evil glint in his eyes.

'Let the Miri go and I promise to ensure that every ship in your fleet would have its hold filled with the best spices of Kozhikode!'

Yusuf heard a gasp from the crew when the words were translated into Portuguese. A greedy gleam in the eyes of each man. He felt like spitting on them with contempt.

But da Gama was unmoved and stood his ground facing al-Faqih, crossing his hands defiantly behind him.

'All right!' al-Faqih continued. 'If you don't believe me, let me offer you a personal assurance. Let the Miri go. I will stay on your ship as hostage while my nephew goes to Kozhikode with the Miri and makes all the necessary arrangements to load your ships with spices.'

Da Gama smiled but made no response. Al-Faqih decided to up the stakes.

'I have more than 300 people on board the Miri. There are women and children and the aged. It is a sin to hold them hostage. I offer myself and assure you that I shall have four of your biggest ships filled with a cargo of spices at my own charge. If this does not get done in two weeks, you can do what you want with me! You have my word!'

Da Gama did not flinch. It was as if a stone wall separated the two men and the Portuguese Admiral couldn't hear what al-Faqih was saying.

Yusuf glanced at the Nakhuda sahib. He was beginning to understand the import of his words. Here was an enemy whose intentions were unknown. How do you negotiate or fight?

'And you can have all the valuables of the Miri! Please!' al-Faqih added, putting in everything he had into the offer.

Da Gama took a deep breath and began to walk away.

'And . . . And . . .' al-Faqih continued, 'I assure you that I can mediate on your behalf with the Samudri Raja of Kozhikode to restore friendly relations between your king and ours!'

Da Gama stopped and turned back. The Portuguese had been trying to get to India for almost a century. To the heart of the spices that they so badly wanted. And it was with much disdain that they discovered, when they arrived five years ago, that the spice trade in India was controlled by the Arabs. People they deeply despised. But the Arabs had the trust of the Indian rulers and in order to oust them, it was necessary for the Portuguese to establish good relations with the Indian kings. The last offer by al-Faqih was a worthy carrot.

A few Portuguese crew members began talking amongst themselves. From their faces, Yusuf could tell that they were dismayed by their captain's silence. Surely the offer al-Faqih was making was too good to be true!

Yusuf reckoned the Portuguese captain was a shrewd businessman, waiting to hear the best the other side had to offer before making a move. He hadn't given anything away, not shown his cards. Meanwhile, al-Faqih had offered everything from gold to spices to political negotiation to himself. There was nothing else he had to put on the table.

The wind howled through the rigging and the sails fluttered.

Several curious eyes watched the two men face off on the deck. Dozens of other sailors lay moaning and groaning on the ship, sick and dying. The Portuguese ships were in need of repair and their men needed to get ashore for food and rest. Surely, Yusuf reckoned, da Gama would take the offer.

'Go back to your ship!' Vasco da Gama finally broke the silence. 'Order your people to hand over everything of value on board! And then I will decide what is to become of you!'

Jauhar al-Faqih held his head up high, his face not reflecting an iota of fear or worry. Taking two paces forward and looking straight into da Gama's eyes, al-Faqih responded, 'When I commanded the ship, they did as I said. Now that you command it, you tell them yourself!'

With that forceful reply, the merchant of Kozhikode turned and walked straight to the boat that would take him back to the Miri. Al-Faqih may have had lost the negotiation but not his honour.

As Yusuf trudged along behind his master, he wondered what else could have been offered. Little did he know that Vasco da Gama did not want spices. Da Gama did not want gold. He wanted blood!

4

BRAVE FACE

'The ship is on fire!' screamed the Nakhuda sahib.

'Quick! Gather all that you can to make a barricade! We have no time!' shouted Yusuf, instructing the quartermaster who was running below deck to fetch some stones from the ballast to use as missiles. He disappeared down the stairway just as a shrapnel whizzed past his ear.

'The women must go below deck!' al-Faqih ordered, ducking to avoid the Portuguese gunfire. 'They ought to be down below with the children!'

Al-Faqih could not bear to see the desperate sight. Over the years, he had dealt with lethal pirates. He had dealt with powerful kings. He had dealt with fearless soldiers and he had dealt with shrewd businessmen. But the Portuguese admiral was none of those.

He was the devil himself.

'I have told them so,' cried the hapless captain, as he hurled another sackful of stones towards the Portuguese longboat. 'But they refuse to listen!' The Nakhuda sahib didn't feel like much of a captain any more. With the Portuguese having stripped the Miri of its rudder and tackle, the vessel had no potential to advance or retreat. She was a sitting duck for the Portuguese to do what they willed.

Tall flames rose high up towards the skies at one end of the ship, which a handful of Portuguese sailors had managed to board and light up with gunpowder.

'Here! Grab this!' Yusuf's mother thrust a bucket into her son's arms, as she joined dozens of passengers scrambling up to douse the flames that were lapping up the sails and the rigging.

'Ummah . . . it isn't safe here on deck for you,' gasped Yusuf, following his mother. 'The master wants all women to go below deck.'

'It's sickening to be down below,' his mother cried, tying a thin towel over her nose to keep the smoke out, 'while you men are fighting here. How can we not join you?'

'And . . . And . . . What about Mariam? Kutti Ahmed? And Uppah?' asked Yusuf, coughing as he progressed against the curtain of flames and smoke.

'They're managing!' she answered, looking heavenward and saying a soft prayer.

Sailors had lined up along the bulwarks, much like soldiers in trenches, positioning themselves to propel stones retrieved from the ship's ballast towards the Portuguese longboats.

It was a battle of two eras. The Portuguese fighting with guns. The Miri fighting back with stones.

'Good Heavens! Suleiman's been hit!' Yusuf screamed looking at the blood splattering out of the helmsman's head. The man was down, a pale vacant look in his eyes. 'Hold on!' Yusuf bent down, pulling him back. 'You'll be fine. You'll be fine.'

'I'll take his place! You look after Suleiman,' said Yusuf's mother, as she prepared to hurl stones with a slingshot she had retrieved from one of the children.

'Ummah . . . you are in the line of fire!' said Yusuf, shielding his mother.

'Oh . . . Come on, now! We can't win this fight if half those on board don't join in!' Yusuf's mother screamed as she rallied the other women on the ship to the frontlines. Some were dousing flames with their scarves and blankets. Others were making barricades with mattresses to keep the fire from spreading. Still others launched stones as projectiles upon the Portuguese.

Since the Portuguese longboats were much smaller in size, stones and sticks rained upon them like a hailstorm and they were forced to retreat. However, more Portuguese boats with reinforcements joined them. They too were met with a hail of missiles hurled by the men and women of the Miri. Soon they backed off.

'Retreating! Retreating! Look! The Portuguese boats are retreating!' yelled the captain in joy, watching the Portuguese boats withdrawing.

The Miri had won.

Only a few days ago, the Miri was a ship returning home with praying pilgrims and laughing children. Now she was a war zone with the dead and the wounded.

Crippled yet defiant, the Miri had managed to fend off the first blow.

But for how long?

5

THE FINAL COUNTDOWN

It had been five days.

The siege on the high seas hadn't ended.

Da Gama watched from his ship. The Miri had fought on too long. *Much longer than expected.*

The Indian ship was strewn with the dead and the injured. Hunger tore through the bellies of those alive as the food on board was running out, their throats parched and dry. *Surely, their determination must run out,* da Gama thought to himself.

'Take all our gold. All our jewels! But spare us!' a woman on board the Miri could be heard crying, leaning over the railings of the quarterdeck.

'What has my baby done to you?' wept another, holding a little infant in her arms. 'How can you attack harmless children?'

'You will burn in hell with the blood of innocent children on your hands!'

'Spare our children!' someone pleaded in desperation, holding up her two-year-old child. 'Kill us if you wish . . . but spare our children!'

'Take these ornaments! Take our gold!' another lady screamed, ripping out the bangles on her wrists and the chain around her neck. 'Take all you want. Just let us go!'

'What a wretched lot!' da Gama spat with contempt. 'Finish them off!'

His orderlies scurried about to implement his instructions. They knew the drill. It wasn't the first time. The gunners were called to their stations. The large ship cannons were readied.

Suddenly, da Gama held up his hand. 'Hold on!' he said, scratching his beard. 'Take away the children. God has given us a chance to redeem those poor souls. Bring them here. And finish off the rest!'

A horn was sounded. Teams were assembled. Instructions were given out.

Da Gama watched from his spy hole. On the Miri, children were snatched away from their parents, babies torn away from their mothers' arms. Every bit of gold and every valuable object taken away.

Babies cried. Children howled. Parents wept.

Da Gama watched and nodded with satisfaction.

Two cannons fired simultaneously as large cannon balls blast out of the Portuguese ship and ripped through the hull of the Miri. The Miri shook. Shards of splintered wood went flying through the air. The mast of the ship cracked into two. The sails were ripped apart.

People could be heard screaming. Howling. Praying for help.

Water began filling the holds of the Miri through the gaping holes in its hull. It slowly began to tilt to one side. And then it began a rapid downward slide, plunging into the cold black ocean.

'Jump!' Yusuf yelled to Mariam. *Where were Uppah and Ummah?* He couldn't see them! 'Hold on to some floating piece of wood!' he screamed. 'That's our only hope!'

Desperate, those on the Miri jumped out as their ship began to sink.

'Pursue them!' da Gama called out, pointing to the people splashing about in the water. 'Strike them with spears! Not one of them must survive!'

The Portuguese soldiers did as they were told. Chasing those swimming and struggling in the water on their boats, they struck them down with spears until they were certain no one could escape. The Admiral's orders were not to be disobeyed. Three hundred lives were snuffed out in minutes.

On the Portuguese ship, da Gama heard the cries of the dying and thanked the Lord. Beside him, the priest prepared for a ceremony as a dozen crying, wailing and petrified Indian children were brought on board.

Kutti Ahmed cried for his mother and wailed all night. But he'd soon forget that horrific night.

For Ahmed was rechristened and renamed Pedro. He'd be taken to a church in Portugal and would dedicate his life to Christ.

Ahmed would soon forget his parents.

Ahmed would soon forget his country.

Ahmed would soon forget the Miri.

History would soon forget the Miri.

History would remember Vasco da Gama as a great explorer.

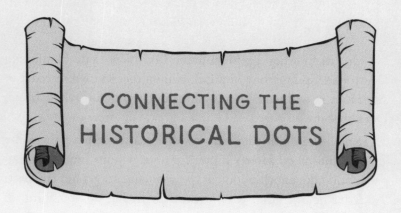

CONNECTING THE HISTORICAL DOTS

 POINT OF VIEW

While India had been trading with Europe since ancient times, the Portuguese were the first Europeans to come to India with the intention to control and rule as a colonial power.

The voyage of Vasco da Gama was hailed by European historians as a major event in exploration and da Gama himself was celebrated as a great explorer.

The Dutch followed the Portuguese. Then came the French. And then the English.

India's history was forever altered by these events.

We in India have often parroted the European version of this story—that Vasco da Gama was a great explorer.

The story of the Miri and many other massacres that took place in India during the voyages of Vasco da Gama however, tell a very different story.

On his first voyage to India in 1498, Vasco da Gama had kidnapped a pilot from Malindi, a town on the eastern coast of Africa. It is with the help of this pilot that he reached India. Does that make Vasco da Gama a great explorer?

The hunter and the lion will obviously not have the same view of the hunt. Here's a point where history requires us to pause and take another look at the way we understand the past.

After hearing the story of the Miri, what do you think of Vasco da Gama?

History has often been used to condition people's minds. You must have come across stories where you have been given only *one* version of events. Often, such stories narrate the positive aspects about those who have written them. The other side is deliberately painted in dark colours. Often, the other side is not known at all, for as the old adage goes—history is written by the *victors*.

When you hear about a historical event, always try to find out the other side of the story. For just like a coin, every story has another side too!

UNBOX THE PAST: FIND HISTORY HIDDEN IN THIS STORY

 ## THE BEGINNING OF A NEW AGE

In the 15th and 16th centuries, the Portuguese set out to create a dramatic new chapter in the history of the world. The Portuguese king sponsored several voyages of discovery in his quest to find the way to India, the source of spices—in particular, pepper.

While several others had made an attempt to round the coast of Africa and make their way to India, the journey was first completed in 1498 by Vasco da Gama, who was then hailed as a great explorer and navigator. Subsequently, every year, several Portuguese ships made their way to India and they even founded what was called the Estado de India (State of India) which was to be their empire in the East. At its height, the Portuguese empire spanned territory from Brazil to Japan.

The Dutch followed the Portuguese. The French and the English joined soon thereafter. This was the beginning of the age of colonization.

 ## KOZHIKODE VS KOCHI: THE EUROPEANS GET A FOOTHOLD

The Portuguese first landed in Kozhikode in 1498. There they found that the spice trade was controlled by the Arabs—people they did not like.

They demanded that the ruler of Kozhikode, known as the Samudri Raja (the Zamorin) expel all Muslims from his kingdom. Hindus, Muslims, Jains, Christians and Jews had all lived harmoniously in Kerala for several centuries and the king found no reason to adhere to the demands of the Portuguese.

The Portuguese then bombarded Kozhikode for refusing to submit to their wishes, killing, plundering and looting. They moved on to Kochi (Cochin), another port slightly south of Kozhikode, whose local ruler was a sworn enemy of the Samudri Raja of Kozhikode. They promised the king of Cochin protection against the Samudri Raja, who was the overlord of Kerala. The king of Cochin was pleased to have a powerful ally against his enemy and allowed the Portuguese to build a fort in Kochi and load their ships with spices.

Thus, the Portuguese used the rivalry between these two kings to gain a foothold in the spice trade and in India.

THE MIRI

The events of the Miri recounted here are true. The ship carrying over 300 civilian passengers, most of whom were returning from a pilgrimage to Mecca, was attacked and drowned by Vasco da Gama in 1503 off the coast of Kerala. The act was completely unprovoked. Moreover, this was one of many similar instances where Portuguese ships attacked and drowned Indians in Indian waters without any reason whatsoever.

 ## INDIA AND THE DISCOVERY OF AMERICA

The Portuguese and the Spanish had been in a race for several years before the arrival of da Gama, to discover a sea route to India, so they could get to the source of the spices. Up until then, since the Arabs and the Venetians controlled the spice trade and by the time the spices reached Western Europe, they cost a lot of money. Hence, they made many attempts to connect directly with India.

One of those many attempts was made by Christopher Columbus, who was convinced that instead of sailing around Africa and going east, if he sailed west instead, he'd reach India faster. At the time, people in Europe were unaware of the existence of the continent of America.

Christopher Columbus requested the monarchs of Portugal, France, England and Spain to fund his expedition and was repeatedly turned down. He was finally given a chance by the king and queen of Spain, for whom he sailed out in 1492. The land Columbus eventually found was not India. However, believing that he had found a sea route to India, the local people were called Indians.

The names *Red Indians or Native Indians,* used for the native people of America, and the name *West Indies,* used for the islands where Columbus actually landed, are remnants of the blunder made by Columbus and the Europeans in their relentless search for India.

 ## PEPPER FOR POTATOES

One of the many fallouts of this era of colonization is culinary in nature, i.e., relating to food. While the Portuguese came to India for her spices, such as pepper, ginger, turmeric, coriander, cinnamon, fennel, etc., a reverse exchange of food also took place. The Portuguese brought along various ingredients and culinary techniques to India.

Potatoes, tomatoes, chillies, maize, guavas, peanuts, papayas and okra are some of the many products that came into India through the Portuguese. Some of these, like the potato, were first discovered by the Portuguese in South America—and spread to the rest of the world on Portuguese ships. Making *pao* (bread), cake and cheese are also methods that were first introduced to India by the Portuguese.

Hence, one finds that names of various food items are common in India and Portugal. For example, *annanas* for pineapple, pao for bread, *batata* for potato, *manga* for mango and so on.

Products like tomatoes, chilies and potatoes are so assimilated into Indian cuisine now that it is impossible to imagine Indian food without them. But these ingredients were not a part of Indian food before the coming of da Gama in the 15th century.

ACKNOWLEDGEMENTS

Thank you, Ahalya Naidu, founder of Trilogy—a wonderful library-cum-bookstore in Mumbai, for leading me to Jumpstart. Thank you, Prashasti Rastogi and the German Book Office for my Jumpstart bridge with Penguin. Thank you Anupam Verma and Arpita Nath, commissioning editors at Penguin, for believing in my work and Shalini Agrawal for fine-toothed combing through the manuscript. Thank you Sai Mandlik for the simple yet eye-catching illustrations that add meaning to the stories and the rest of the awesome team at Penguin that gave this book their very best. Thank you Sumathi Sridhar and Lakshmi Vaidyalingam for racking your brains over the title and for other timely inputs.

Appa, Amma, Athai, Shashi, Karthik & Kabir—words cannot express my gratitude. Everything I am and will be, is because *you* make it possible.